You Complicate Me

Isabel Jordan

Cover design by Dar Albert, Wicked Smart Designs

ISBN-10: 1986937992
ISBN-13: 9781986937993

DEDICATION

To L.E. Wilson, for what probably totaled hours of cover help and beta reading (and re-reading and re-reading). Without your support, I'd still be agonizing over font.

ACKNOWLEDGMENTS

I'd love to say no one helped with this book and that I did it all by myself, using only my talent, wit, and skills. (Bwahahahahah!!!!) But, yeah, that's totally not the case.

First of all, thanks to, Connor, for just being yourself. You're a beautiful, smart, funny kid who sometimes drives me absolutely crazy, and that's OK.

Thanks to my husband, Don. No one has done more than you have to help me achieve my dreams. Don't think I haven't noticed.

Big thanks to my parents for their continued support and encouragement. (Watch out for black ice!)

Thanks to the all-kinds-of-awesome Dar Albert at Wicked Smart Designs for my GORGEOUS cover art. Seriously, you're magic!

HUGE thanks to Renee Wright for your eagle proofreading and editing eye yet again. You've preserved what little dignity I have left soooooo many times.

Thanks to LE Wilson, beta reader extraordinaire. (See dedication)

And last by certainly not least, thank you to all the wonderful readers out there who have stuck with me since 2014 when I released my first little paranormal romance, *Semi-Charmed.* (Extra big thanks to my peeps in the Bitch, Write Faster group! *waves enthusiastically*) Your support means more to me than you'll ever know.

Chapter One

In retrospect, the Valium probably would've been enough to soothe Grace Montgomery's nerves on the flight from Los Angeles to Indianapolis. The wine was most likely overkill.

As was the tequila.

It had all started innocently enough. "Take one pill an hour before the flight," her doctor had told her, "and one an hour into the flight. You'll be completely relaxed. Valium is magic, I swear."

"The kind of magic that keeps planes from falling from the sky in a ball of fiery death?" Grace had asked.

Her doctor's answering smirk should've been a warning. "The kind of magic that makes you not care on the way down."

And she hadn't. Cared, that is. The magic Valium had done its job.

Until take-off, at least.

As soon as the plane started rolling down the runway, as soon as she felt the rumbling of the engine in her belly, she started panicking. The man sitting next to her in seat C2, no doubt having noticed the white-knuckled grip she had on their adjoining armrest, had suggested a glass of wine, which she'd requested from the flight attendant as soon as she'd been allowed. But even though she gulped it down in two swallows, the wine was absolutely no match for her anxiety, because she soon started hyperventilating.

C2 had pressed an air-sickness bag into one of her hands, and a mini bottle of tequila into the other. After breathing deeply into the bag for a few moments, she'd unscrewed the tequila and downed it, too. One swallow that time.

Grace was nothing if not a quick learner.

It was then she'd made what she thought was a tragic error. She'd asked for a second bottle of tequila, which she used to wash down her second Valium. The calm that had quickly washed over her was amazing. She couldn't remember a time when she'd felt so relaxed.

And warm. She was suddenly really, really, warm. So it only made sense that she'd strip off her sweater, right?

Sadly, while she was shedding layers, she elbowed the guy next to her in the eye.

"Jesus Christ," he'd muttered, holding a hand over one eye.

That was when she got her first good look at C2.

Maybe it was the Valium, or maybe it was the alcohol, but holy hell, he was *beautiful.*

His inky hair was long overdue for a trim and fell in messy disarray—the kind of messy disarray that hot men achieved naturally and women paid big bucks to a salon to fake—to just above the collar of his white button-down shirt. With his knife-edged cheekbones, strong jaw, and olive complexion, he looked like he could be Hugh Jackman's younger brother.

Grace had watched *Wolverine* four times, and not because the storyline was stellar (or even remotely plausible, really). Her mouth immediately went dry. Other parts of her…not so much.

"I'm r-really sorry," she whispered.

He lowered his hand and she winced at the elbow-sized welt forming under his eye. "Are you always like this on a plane?" he asked.

"Like what?"

"Fucking crazy?"

She frowned at him. "I'm a nervous flyer, okay? Lots of people are nervous flyers."

He shook his head and ran his hand through that amazing hair of his. "This isn't nervous. I've seen nervous. You're a train wreck, lady."

He wasn't lying. Didn't make his comment any less insulting. "I'm sorry if my fear of falling from the sky and plummeting to a fiery death is inconveniencing you in any way."

One black brow winged upward. "Fear all you want. I couldn't care less. But when you try to blind me with your fucking elbow while you strip down to your underwear…well, that's when I start to care."

Grace glanced down at her white layering tank top. It wasn't see-through. Minimal cleavage was on display. Perfectly respectable. "I said I was sorry about elbowing you, okay? And I'm not in my underwear."

His gaze dipped down. "I can tell that you're cold." He smirked as his eyes met hers again. "Or turned on."

She *so* wasn't cold.

"I'm cold," she said dryly. "Don't flatter yourself."

His smirk morphed into a full-fledged grin, and Grace fought the urge to fan herself. Jesus, the grin was nothing short of panty-dropping. A smile like that should be illegal. All those straight white teeth and the dimple that carved into his cheek…it was gratuitous, really.

And his eyes? An amazing oceanic mix of blue and pale green. Men shouldn't be allowed to have eyes that pretty.

"Let's start over," he said. He held out his hand. "I'm Nick. Nick O'Connor."

She was so busy staring at his eyes—and being envious of his thick, dark eyelashes, if she was being honest with herself— that it took her a moment to realize he was speaking to her. She took his hand. "Grace. Grace Montgomery."

Something akin to recognition lit his eyes for a moment, making her wonder if he knew her. Had they met before? But she immediately dismissed the thought. If she'd met *this* guy before, she'd remember it.

His hand was warm and callused, and dwarfed hers. Her gaze traveled from his hand up his thick forearm, exposed by the rolled-up sleeve of his shirt. His biceps strained the fabric of that shirt, as well. If the arms were any indication, a muscly chest and flat stomach were a foregone conclusion.

She considered then that her judgment might be impaired. No one was *this* good-looking. Or else Nick O'Connor was genetically blessed in a way that was totally unfair to all other men.

Tequila goggles. She was wearing a set of tequila goggles. There was no other explanation.

He cleared his throat, drawing her attention back to his face. He let go of her hand and she fought the urge to grab his again. She knew she was an embarrassment to feminists everywhere, but there was something insanely comforting about having a big, strong guy holding her hand. If she'd grabbed him early on, maybe she wouldn't have needed the Valium. Or wine. Or tequila.

"So, Grace," he said, "have you always been a nervous flyer?"

She laid her head back against the seat, suddenly feeling a

little off balance. "Yeah. I don't like being closed in. Or depending on people I don't know to fly the plane. And land the plane."

"Uh huh. So you're one of *those*."

She frowned at him again. "One of those *what*?"

"Control freaks."

"I am not a control freak."

Was it her imagination, or had she slurred that sentence?

He gave her the panty-dropping grin again. Yep, she'd slurred.

"Whatever you say, angel."

Being called a control freak was kind of a hot button for Grace. It was something her ex-husband never failed to bring up when they'd argued, which had been often. And the fact that this total stranger would agree with her ex pissed her off. She also took exception to him assigning her a nickname. Grace unbuckled her seatbelt and stood up to tell him so.

And that's when her memory got a little…fuzzy.

She had a distinct memory of poking him in the chest, telling him he didn't know anything about her. He'd told her to sit down. To *calm* down. She'd refused, colorfully and loudly. She'd tried to badger a man in another row into trading seats with her. The guy had refused, colorfully and loudly.

Nick had gotten in the middle of that argument and tried to tell her something about who he was, what his job was, but she was too busy yelling about…something to catch all of it.

The next thing she knew, Nick had forced her back into her seat. He might've also threatened to cuff her if she got into any other arguments with passengers, which seemed a little excessive. And…kinky.

"I'm sorry," she thought he'd said at that point.

"I'm sorry, too," she vaguely remembered responding.

Then, she couldn't be sure, but she thought she might have leaned over and puked all over his shoes. After that…there was nothing but blissful, blissful unconsciousness.

Chapter Two

Nick watched Grace through the two-way mirror in the interrogation room/holding cell at the Indianapolis airport. Her long, golden blonde hair frizzed around her heart-shaped face like a tangled halo. Those amazing moss-green eyes of hers were bloodshot and at half-mast as she rested her pale forehead on her palm. He'd be willing to bet she felt like hell.

"Grace Emerson Montgomery," Walden Carroll said from behind him, reading the contents of a manila file folder. "Age twenty-seven, five-foot-six, one-thirty."

Since Nick had carried her off the plane, he was all too familiar with her weight, and it was *perfect.* Grace had an amazing body.

"She works in LA as a corporate attorney," Walden said. "Never had so much as a traffic ticket. Hardly looks like a terrorist, Nick."

Even terrorists didn't usually look like terrorists, Nick thought. And this dumbass, wannabe air marshal would know that if he'd been on the job for more than a nanosecond. Or if he'd ever been up to his ass in *real* terrorists in Afghanistan like Nick had.

"I know she's not a terrorist, Walden," he said patiently. "She was drunk and disorderly. I only threatened to cuff her to settle her down and keep her from upsetting the other passengers."

Walden smirked. "I wouldn't mind cuffing her."

Nick fought a sudden urge to knock a few of Walden's teeth down his throat. "Down, boy," he muttered, not sure if he'd meant the comment for Walden or for himself. "I didn't haul her in here for my own amusement."

"Yeah, whatever." Walden pressed the file into Nick's hand. "I'm out of here. She's all yours. Don't do anything I wouldn't do. Or then again…" He waggled his eyebrows in a manner he probably thought was provocative, but actually made him look like he had Tourette's.

Nick didn't glance at him, but did take the time to give him the finger. Walden chuckled and let himself out.

Looking through the file Walden had put together on Grace, he noted she was a Notre Dame grad. Impressive.

Nick was always amazed by people who possessed the mental fortitude to make it through college. He'd barely made it through high school. He'd joined the military as soon as he graduated, then from there, went into a line of work that required more muscle, skill, and instinct than book smarts.

Smart good girls like Grace Montgomery historically had little use for Jersey trailer trash like Nick. If they didn't need a quick meaningless fuck or the perfect guy to piss off their rich daddies, Nick was accustomed to having girls like Grace look right through him.

That was okay with Nick, though. Sure, it had stung a bit when he was a kid, but he was over it now. Mostly. And besides, really smart women were often fairly *complicated.* Complicated women usually either came with or caused drama, and Nick had a *very* low tolerance for that kind of bullshit.

And once she found out why his travel plans were so in sync with hers, he had a feeling things with Grace were going to get *extra* complicated.

With a resigned sigh, Nick walked into the interrogation room, file in one hand, bottle of water and three aspirins in the other. Grace barely moved. Her only acknowledgment of his presence was a brief upward flick of her eyelashes. He slapped the file down on the chipped Formica table in front of her, causing her to flinch.

"Hello again, Grace."

"Uh huh."

He chuckled. "Got a bit of a headache, I take it?"

She lifted her head and shot him the look of death. He grinned at her, then handed her the water bottle and aspirins.

Grace fell on those pills like a starving woman on a steak dinner. "Oh, thank God," she muttered, then tossed the pills back dry.

Nick raised a brow at her. She shrugged. "I never can twist those caps off." She held up a slender, white hand. "Girly wuss hands."

Yeah, he could think of a few good uses for those girly wuss hands. He could just imagine them trailing over his chest, down his abdomen, slowly reaching lower to wrap around his…

He gave himself a sharp mental slap across the face. *Pull yourself together, man.*

He grabbed the bottle and twisted the top off for her. She accepted it and took a few greedy swallows.

"Take it easy," he said. "Don't want you getting sick again."

Grace wiped a drop of water off her bottom lip with the back of her hand and closed her eyes. "I threw up on your shoes, didn't I?"

"Yep."

She dropped her forehead to the table. "Oh, God," she groaned.

"Aw, don't worry about it. You're not the first to puke on me."

She lifted her head an inch or so. "Really?"

"Really." When she looked relieved, he couldn't help but add,

"You were the first unconscious passenger I had to fireman-carry off a plane, though. Thanks for that. It was interesting."

"Oh, God."

He laughed as her forehead hit the table again. "Seriously, Grace, don't be embarrassed. I doubt I could've handled two tequilas, a glass of wine, and two Valiums—and I'm eight inches taller and sixty pounds heavier than you."

"I'm sure you're just saying that to make me feel better, but thank you."

"You're welcome."

She lifted her head and glanced down at herself, just then seeming to notice that her slumped posture put a healthy amount of cleavage on display. "Jesus," she muttered. "You couldn't have told me my breasts are on the table?"

He probably should have. A gentleman would have. But Nick wasn't much of a gentleman, and her breasts on the table were the best thing he'd seen all day, so he kept his mouth shut.

Grace rolled her eyes. "This is why I'm off men," she said to no one in particular.

He leaned forward. "Giving girls a try?" he asked, injecting a hopeful note in his voice.

"Ugh. No."

"Well, that's just disappointing." He shot her another grin as she frowned at him.

"Am I being charged with anything?"

He shook his head. "Honestly, I wasn't even officially on duty on that flight, and I feel a little bad about the whole thing. I shouldn't have suggested the alcohol. Not my most professional moment, you know? I really am sorry about that."

"It's not your fault. I should've known better. I panicked."

She had a really great voice, he noticed. Sweet and low-pitched, whiskey-smooth. "Did you rent a car for the trip to River Oak, or is someone coming to get you?"

Grace blinked at him. "How do you know where I'm going?" Then her eyes widened, and she asked, incredulous, "Does the Department of Homeland Security know where *everyone* on the plane is going?"

He laughed. "No, Grace. We don't know everyone's travel plans. I just happen to know yours."

"How?"

"Guess you were too panicked on the flight to pick up on my last name."

He could practically see the wheels turning in that pretty little head of hers. When the truth hit her, she groaned and dropped her head back to her hands. "Jesus Christ. Really?"

Nick leaned forward and smirked as he held out his hand. "Let's start over. Hi, I'm Nick O'Connor, and in a week, I'm going to be your brother-in-law. Can I call you sis?"

Chapter Three

Sweet merciful crap.

Grace was still struggling with the realization that she'd been carried off a plane by an air marshal. An air marshal whose sister was marrying her little brother. An air marshal she'd be seeing at every major family gathering until the end of time—or at least until the crazy kids who were getting married way too young got a divorce.

But all that wasn't even *nearly* as embarrassing as the X-rated Wolverine fantasies she'd had about Nick O'Connor since she elbowed him in the eye. And yes, that was fantasi*es*, as in plural.

Now, in the passenger seat of a rented Escape that sounded like it was begging for mercy every time Nick hit the gas, heading into deadlocked traffic on what was obviously the highway of the damned, Grace contemplated why she'd agreed when he suggested they ride together. She decided to blame the residual tequila/wine/Valium in her bloodstream for this misstep in her normally impeccable judgment.

Well, okay, her judgment wasn't *impeccable*. But hell, it wasn't usually *this* bad.

"It's not all that bad, you know."

She jumped at the sound of his voice. "Beg pardon?"

He glanced over at her, then back at the line of cars in front of them. "You look completely forlorn over there. So you had a few Wolverine fantasies about your future brother-in-law. So what? It's not like we're blood relation."

Grace was pretty sure her jaw hit the Escape's leather seat. "What?" she screeched.

He didn't look at her again, but that dimple—that truly annoying dimple that seemed to only pop out when he was laughing at her—made another appearance. "You talk a lot when you're drunk, Grace."

She groaned and slammed her head back against the seat. "Jesus, could this get any more embarrassing?"

"You also groped my ass when I had you slung over my shoulder, carrying you off the plane," he added helpfully.

Embarrassment had struck her mute, she decided, because when she opened her mouth, no sound came out.

His gaze slid to hers, and his smile was pure sin. "I might've groped yours a little, too, if it makes you feel better."

She sputtered. "It most certainly does *not*."

He lifted a shoulder. "Oh, well, I won't hold a grudge if you don't. Bygones and all."

Bygones. Grace took a deep breath and counted to ten under her breath. "Are you purposefully trying to embarrass and irritate me?"

"A little, yeah."

His truthful answer stunned her silent for another brief moment. "Why?" she finally managed to ask.

"You've been silent for about forty miles." He shrugged again. "I was bored."

"You were *bored.*"

"Yep."

"And antagonizing me entertains you?"

He cursed as traffic forced him to stop again, then met her incredulous gaze and smiled. "Yeah. You get all pink and squinty-eyed. It's sexy."

Grace blinked. She wasn't sure anyone had ever called her sexy before. Her apple cheeks and the dusting of pale freckles across her nose usually got her lumped into the *cute* category. With the right amount of makeup and good lighting she could pull off *pretty*. But sexy? Never.

And certainly not by men who looked like Nick O'Connor.

The type of guy she usually ended up with was more Seth Rogan than Hugh Jackman. Not that there was anything wrong with Seth Rogan. His work in *The Green Hornet* was highly underrated in her opinion.

In truth, men like Nick—the kind who oozed testosterone and sex—always made Grace a little nervous. She imagined he'd been a jock in high school. Homecoming King. Voted most likely to take the head cheerleader's virginity.

Grace had been captain of the debate team. Class treasurer. Voted most likely to die a virgin.

That last one had stung a bit at the time.

She realized she was staring at him and shifted her gaze back out the window. She'd been a little disappointed when he walked into the interrogation room. She'd hoped that when she sobered up, Nick would be less…well, *less*.

Sadly, he wasn't.

The only imperfection he seemed to have—other than his personality and apparent love of torturing her—was a faint scar that ran down his left temple. "How'd you get your scar?"

His smile disappeared. "Afghanistan. IED."

Grace waited for him to elaborate. He didn't.

He obviously didn't want to talk about it. She'd only asked because she was groping for something, *anything*, that would make him less attractive. To her way of thinking, if he was less attractive, maybe she wouldn't be so embarrassed about the giant ass she made of herself when she met him.

But her plan backfired, because knowing he'd been injured in the line of duty while serving his country instead of, say, wrecking his car while driving drunk, just made her feel like a bitch of epic proportions for even bringing the scar up. "I'm sorry," she murmured. "I shouldn't have asked. And thank you for your service."

"Fair question," he said, not really sounding offended. "Scar's kind of hard to miss. And you're welcome."

In the awkward silence that followed, Grace decided it was time to lighten the mood, so she said, "You know, I once read a Liverpool and Stirling study on the attractiveness of facial scars to the opposite sex. They found that men with facial scars were 5.7 percentage points higher in terms of physical appeal than men without any scars."

One black brow lifted. "Really? 5.7 percentage points, huh?"

She nodded. "It's a fact. And, of course, I have my own personal experience to go on."

"And what experience might that be?"

"I showed Bobby Jorgenson my appendix scar in the seventh grade. His direct quote: 'that's *so* hot'."

He chuckled, and Grace felt an irrational surge of warmth at the sound. "I'd have to say good old Bobby was probably referring to your body, not your scar," he said. Then he glanced over at her and wiggled his brows comically while adding, "Although I'd need to see it to be sure."

She smiled. "Now *there's* the Clarence-Thomas-like letch I've so enjoyed in our short time together. Welcome back."

"Wow, love the Clarence Thomas reference. You could've gone for an obvious Weinstein reference, but you went with a classic. I appreciate that."

"Yeah, well, smart girls are usually into the classics, and I'm *very* smart," she joked.

"I noticed."

And didn't sound entirely pleased about it, if she hadn't missed her guess. Maybe he preferred dumb bimbos. He wouldn't be the first, she thought sourly. Her husband had left her for a dumb bimbo with Cheeto-colored skin, giant silicone double-D's, and a tongue stud.

"So tell me about your brother," Nick said.

Grace smiled. "Michael's great. You'll love him. Everyone does."

Nick snorted. "He's banging my little sister. I doubt I'll love him. I'm sure I can tolerate him, though, as long as he's good to her."

Grace stiffened. "Hey, I'm not really loving the idea of the little brother I read *Goodnight Moon* to every night until he was ten *banging* anyone, either. But it's a two-way street. She's banging him, too. At least he's marrying her."

His noncommittal grunt told her he was just as thrilled about the two nineteen-year-olds getting married as she was. "Is he like you?"

"He's open and outgoing and creative—he's an artist—and a total optimist…so, no, he's not anything like me."

"Not a Valium-and-tequila kind of guy?"

She sighed. "I'm never going to live that down, am I?"

His mouth quirked up. "Nope. It was the high point of my career."

Stupid amazing-looking smart-assed man, she thought.

"What about you, angel? I know you're a fancy corporate lawyer, and I've heard all about your *awesome* family from my sister," he said, adopting a silly soprano lilt on the word *awesome.* "But tell me about you. Is there some big burly boyfriend who's going to kick my ass for groping yours?"

Grace laughed out loud. "No. No boyfriend. I have an ex-husband, but he certainly won't be defending my honor anytime soon."

Brad simply wasn't the honor-defending type. Harvard grads

were too dignified for that. He'd expect her to defend her own honor.

"What happened with that?"

"He met someone he liked better."

Nick frowned. "He sounds like a dumbass."

Hearing that felt better than it should have. "Well, I don't call him doucheBrad for nothing."

He chuckled. "At least you're not bitter."

She really wasn't. Not anymore, at least. After an initial bout of anger—during which she burned piles of his Brooks Brothers suits in their backyard barbeque pit like a jilted lover from a bad Lifetime movie—she was willing to admit to herself that she and Brad had been growing apart for a long time. If they'd ever really been *together* in their four years of marriage, that is.

Looking at it objectively, she was actually a little relieved that he'd walked out first. Chesty Cheeto had most likely saved her a long, uncomfortable talk when it came right down to it. And at least doucheBrad had the decency to tell her the truth when he started schtupping his dumb bimbo.

"Apparently it was my fault," she said dryly. "I'm emotionally closed-off. Or so I'm told."

"Oh, hey," he said, holding a hand out to her as if they were meeting for the first time. "I'm a commitment-phobe. Or so *I'm* told."

Grace shook his hand once, laughing at his equally desert-dry tone. "So you've been labeled, too. Why is that? Why doesn't anyone ever say, 'Oh, she just hasn't found anyone she wants to open up to.' Or, 'he just hasn't met the right girl yet.' Why is it always our fault?"

He shook his head. "No clue. Nice to know we live in the same emotional neighborhood, though."

"Yeah. Maybe we can carpool during our next breakup."

"That'd be *great*."

Grace couldn't help but smile. "So, what about you? Is there some six-foot-tall, Barbie-looking glamazon out there who is going to kick my ass for groping yours?"

"Nope," he answered, turning those amazing eyes on her just long enough to cause her heart rate to kick up a notch or two. "I'm unencumbered."

Typical guy answer, she thought, suppressing an eye roll. He made having a relationship sound as appealing as having a noose around the neck. Or hemorrhoids. "Hard to believe."

"I know, right?"

He smiled at her again and Grace shifted uncomfortably in her seat. Bastard had at least a hundred different smiles, and each one made her slightly wetter than the last. If she could harness the power of any one of Nick's smiles and sell it to lonely women on eBay, she'd never have to write another legal brief as long as she lived.

"Tell me about your sister. Michael never tells me anything about his personal life anymore. I know my parents have met her, but I haven't even seen a picture of her."

"Sadie's the sweetest kid you'll ever meet. Everyone loves her. She's a journalism student. The first kid in the O'Connor family to go to college."

Adoration and pride was clear in his voice. She'd be willing to bet Nick had been a great big brother. The kind who'd beat the crap out of anyone who hurt his little sister. Grace envied Sadie. She'd always wanted a big brother. Michael was awesome and she wouldn't trade him for anything in the world, but as the older sibling, she'd always taken care of him. It would've been nice to have someone looking out for her.

"What the fuck," Nick muttered as traffic ground to a standstill again.

Grace pulled her cell phone out of her purse. "I'll call my cousin. He's probably an hour ahead of us. I bet he'll know what's going on."

"What?" Gage growled into the phone when he picked up on the third ring.

Grace smirked. "I take it you're stuck in traffic as well, dear cousin?"

"Jesus," he muttered. "I've been sitting here for over an hour. I think I heard a helicopter a minute ago. Must be a bad accident. I feel kind of guilty."

"Why would you feel guilty?"

"Because about twenty minutes ago, I said, 'Someone better be dead, because if this is just construction traffic, I'll be seriously pissed.'"

"Well, you're a terrible person," she said, knowing all the while she probably would've said the same thing, and probably *did* the last time she'd been stuck in traffic in LA. "So where are you?"

"Fuck if I know. I think I passed a little town called Jericho a while ago. I'm not sure, though. Everything looks the same when it's surrounded by corn."

Grace glanced out the window. "Apparently, Indiana is part of something called the Corn Belt, which is basically just a fancy name for an area where the conditions are perfect for growing corn."

Gage snorted. "Where do you even get that shit?"

"I read something other than medical journals and porn," she replied tartly.

He grumbled something unintelligible, but she ignored it and said, "I think the fields are beautiful. I can see why Michael chose to go to school here."

Another snort from Gage. Grumpy bastard, she thought. Grace glanced at Nick. "Gage says he passed a town called Jericho a while ago. He's been sitting in traffic ever since."

Nick let his head drop back against the seat. "Grace, we're hell and gone from Jericho. With the rate we're moving, we won't get to the resort until tomorrow."

Grace bit back a nasty curse word she generally saved for special occasions. "Great. Gage, I don't think we'll be there tonight. If you get there before us, will you tell everyone we're on our way?"

"Who's 'we'?"

"I'm with Nick O'Connor, brother of the bride." There was a loaded pause. "I'll explain tomorrow," she added wryly.

"Yes, you will. And get there as quick as you can. Don't leave me stranded with those people."

Grace laughed. "*Those people* are your family."

"Doesn't make them any less annoying. Besides, you know you're my favorite."

"Aw, I'm touched."

"And sarcastic. Don't forget sarcastic."

"Never. Love you."

"Yeah, me, too."

Grace disconnected the call, then shoved the phone back in her purse. "So what do you recommend we do, marshal?"

He ran a hand through his hair, leaving it sticking up in the front in a way that should've looked ridiculous. Instead, it gave him a just-fucked look that made Grace cross her legs. Tight.

"Well, the sun's going down, and it doesn't look like traffic will be moving again anytime soon. I don't know about you, but I'm exhausted. I say we get the hell off the highway of the damned at the first opportunity and don't get anywhere near it again until morning. What do you say? Dinner and a hotel?"

A meal and a good night's sleep sounded like heaven to Grace. "Let's do it."

He glanced over at her, brows raised. Then she realized the double meaning of her statement and rolled her eyes. "Oh, grow up," she muttered.

Nick chuckled. "Whatever you say, angel. Whatever you say."

Chapter Four

Exit 41 boasted a gas station with an attached diner, a bail bond office, and a motel with a flashing neon vacancy sign. Or, at least Nick assumed it said vacancy. It was hard to tell with so many letters burned out.

Since the place wasn't even on the map, Nick assumed Exit 41 existed solely for the benefit of long-haul truckers and other travelers. All he knew for sure was that the closest real town was twenty miles and an hour in traffic past the limits of his patience. Stopping elsewhere wasn't really an option at this point.

Nick parked the car in front of the diner and glanced over at Grace, half expecting her to refuse to go inside. After all, a high-priced attorney in LA probably didn't spend much time in places like Nadine's Eat Here and Get Gas. But Grace surprised him by throwing the door open and practically leaping from the car.

"Thank God," she said on a huge sigh. "I'm *starving*."

He managed to grab the door for her, but only a heartbeat before she would've tugged it open herself.

An air-conditioned blast of fried-food-scented air smacked Nick in the face as soon as he followed Grace into the diner. His mouth instantly watered. Apparently he was starving, too.

The inside of the diner was a pleasant surprise. The black Formica tabletops were spotless, and the red vinyl booths and stainless-steel counter gleamed under the fluorescent lighting. Not at all what he expected of a truck stop diner.

A heavyset, forty-ish woman with a mop of brick-red curls and a nametag that proclaimed her Nadine greeted them with a wide, gap-toothed grin. "Hi, there," she said. "Table or booth?"

"Booth," Nick answered.

"Sure thing, handsome."

They followed Nadine to a booth at the back of the diner. Nick sidestepped Grace to get the seat that faced the door. No self-respecting ex-Marine would ever sit with his back to the door. Grace glanced at him with a question in her eyes, but didn't seem to mind too much as she took a seat across from him.

"Drinks?" Nadine asked as she handed them two laminated menus.

"Coke," Grace said. "Regular, please."

Nick ordered the same and turned his attention back to Grace when Nadine shuffled back to the kitchen.

"So," Nick began, "tell me who I'll be meeting this week."

"Well, other than my brother and cousin, my mom and dad, Sarah and David, will be there. They live out in Seattle. She's an accountant and he's an actuary. They're, um, well-meaning."

He leaned forward. “Interesting choice of words.”

She blew a wayward curl off her forehead. “Oh, don’t get me wrong, they’re great people. They’re just unique.”

She didn’t explain and he didn’t push. He supposed he’d figure out what she meant soon enough.

“Then, I imagine dad will dig up Grandma Ruthie and drag her out here,” she added. “She’s a joy.”

Her tone dripped sarcasm, but as Grace spoke, it became clear that she adored and was exasperated by her family in equal measure. He envied her that. His own family was a bit of a joke, as Grace would soon find out. If any of them bothered to show, that is.

“Well, Sadie is really impressed with everyone she’s met,” he said. “In fact, she can’t stop talking about them. I’ve heard more about your family than I’ve heard about Michael.”

A frown line creased her smooth brow. “That’s kind of weird, isn’t it? Wouldn’t you think she’d be talking about Michael nonstop?”

He shrugged. “I wouldn’t know. Never been married or engaged.”

Nadine returned with their drinks. “You kids decide what you’d like?”

Nick nodded to Grace. “Go ahead, angel.”

She paused for a moment, giving him a look he couldn't interpret. Then, she sighed and turned her attention to Nadine. "Okay, I'll have a bacon double cheeseburger with fries…no, wait, onion rings…no, wait, fries *and* onion rings. And a side salad with a cup of chicken tortilla soup. And a large chocolate shake." She shrugged sheepishly, then added, "Please."

"Okay," Nadine said, dragging the word out a few extra syllables. She turned to Nick with wide eyes. "What about you, doll?"

"Uh, I'll have a cup of beef vegetable and a turkey club, please. Thanks, Nadine."

As Nadine shuffled back to the kitchen, Nick looked back to Grace, who was gnawing on her thumbnail. "What's the matter?" he asked her.

For a moment, he thought she'd avoid answering, but eventually, she said, in a low voice, "I have a really fast metabolism, so I'm hungry all the time. It's embarrassing, okay? I try not to eat in front of new people if I can help it. But I get sick if I don't eat every few hours, so I didn't have a choice this time."

Nick had seen her drunk, pissed off, and throwing attitude at him like a major-league pitcher, but seeing her looking all nervous and vulnerable sucker-punched him.

He reached across the table and grabbed her hand. "Hey, you don't have to be embarrassed about anything with me, okay? Just be yourself. I like *everything* I've seen so far."

She blinked at him, then glanced at his hand on hers. "Thanks," she whispered.

And as her eyes lifted to his again, the air around them shifted. In that moment, Nick wanted nothing more than to lean across the table and find out if her lush pink lips were as soft as they looked.

Grace broke eye contact first, gently pulling her hand back to her lap.

Too intense too fast, Nick thought. He'd made her uncomfortable. *Nicely done, asshole.*

Time to lighten the mood.

"Besides, your body rocks, so if you need to eat 5,000 calories a day to keep it, I'm all for it."

Her surprised laughed ended in a snort, and Nick chuckled as she slapped a hand over her mouth. "Relax, Grace. It's just you and me."

Grace really wanted to relax, but she just didn't see how that was possible when one touch from Nick sent electricity through her whole body. Okay, maybe not through her *whole* body. More like from his fingertips straight to lady land. There was just no relaxing around a man that, well, *manly*.

And for a moment, right before she totally wussed out and broke eye contact, she'd been sure he was going to kiss her. She now knew his eyes darkened to midnight blue when things got intense. Damned if she wasn't stupid enough to want to see it again, too.

Nadine arrived, almost staggering under the weight of the tray she carried. Nick jumped up immediately and helped her distribute the plates. She thanked him profusely before heading up front to greet a young mother and child who'd just walked in.

Grace dug into her food enthusiastically, partially because she was starving, but also to distract herself from thinking about how hot Nick had looked when he brushed off Nadine's thanks. He'd looked almost embarrassed by her gratitude.

Everything was a lot simpler for her when she thought he was just a good-looking, smug jerk who took pleasure in making her uncomfortable. The fact that he was a nice guy who just happened to look like a god was a little more than Grace could handle.

Grace grabbed the ketchup and created a little moat around her fries and onion rings. "So, you've heard all about me. What about you?"

"What do you want to know?"

His tone could only be described as cautious. If they were in a deposition, she'd say he was hiding something. She decided to lob him a softball question instead of leading with her wicked curve. "How did you become an air marshal?"

He shrugged. "Job options are somewhat limited for a guy fresh out of the Marines with no college degree and a questionable skill set."

"That's an interesting word choice. What is a questionable skill set, exactly?"

"The things I've been good at in my life, you can't make money on legally."

She paused with a fry halfway to her mouth. Did he mean…?

He chuckled. "Get your mind out of the gutter, angel. I wasn't talking about sex."

"Oh." Well, that was vaguely disappointing.

"But now that you mention it…" he trailed off, winking at her before taking a bite of his sandwich.

Grace popped the fry in her mouth so he wouldn't see her with a slack jaw. Again.

"Seriously, though," Nick continued, "I was a sniper. There's not much market for that here in the States."

She chewed thoughtfully for a moment. "I find that hard to believe. Marine snipers are some of the best in the world. I'm sure

SWAT teams would fist-fight over you."

"Maybe before this," he said dryly, tapping the scar on his temple with his index finger. "Now? Not so much. I lost a little peripheral vision in the explosion, which means I wouldn't make a good sniper."

"Oh. Sorry," she muttered. She felt awful. This was the second time she'd brought up his injury.

"It's OK," he said, snatching one of her fries before she could object. "My overall vision is still good, and my marksmanship is better than most." He shrugged. "I like my job. I get to travel to places I'd never be able to otherwise afford. Meet the most interesting people."

Nick grinned at her again. He really needed to stop doing that, Grace decided. If she got any hotter, she was bound to set off the sprinklers in the building.

"What about you?" he asked. "What made you want to become a lawyer?"

She broke an onion ring in half and dragged it through the ketchup moat. "When I was in the third grade, my teacher told me that Christopher Columbus discovered America."

His brow furrowed as he stirred his soup. "And that made you want to be a lawyer?"

She frowned at him. "Do you want to hear this story or not, Mr. Impatient Pants?"

He chuckled quietly. "Sorry. Continue. Please."

"So my question to her was, how could Christopher Columbus have discovered America when there were already people living here?"

He smiled. "That's a great question. What was her answer?"

"She told me to stop being sassy and made me stand in the corner for the rest of the class."

He shook his head and winced. "I'm betting she regretted that."

"You know it. I went directly to the library after school and checked out every book I could find about Christopher Columbus. It didn't take long to find out that Vikings had landed on American soil long before Columbus." She popped the onion ring in her mouth and chewed it up before continuing. "So even if it was possible to 'discover' something that already belonged to someone else, Christopher Columbus *certainly* hadn't been the first."

"And I'm guessing you laid this all out for your teacher."

"Yep. And not only did she admit she was wrong, but I made her apologize for sticking me in the corner. It was my first victory, and let me tell you, it felt *good*." Grace shook her head, grinning. "I've been arguing ever since. Becoming a lawyer was the most natural career move in the world for me."

He leaned forward and she mimicked his action instinctively. His voice lowered as he said, "So, Grace Emerson Montgomery, just how good are you?"

Her tongue stuck to the roof of her mouth and she felt the blush start somewhere around her toes and shoot right up to her hairline.

He studied her for a moment. "Right to the gutter again, huh, angel?" He shook his head. "I do love the way you think. But I was asking how good you are as a *lawyer*."

She instantly relaxed. "I'm the best."

"Yeah?" he asked. "So, you always win in court? Get people to confess and shit, like *A Few Good Men*?"

She laughed at the enthusiasm in his tone. "No, nothing like that. I've never done any criminal work. My clients are big companies, and if they have to go to court, it probably means I really failed them." She popped another fry into her mouth. "And I do my best to make sure I *never* fail them."

"And you're happy?"

Grace blinked. She wasn't sure anyone had ever asked her that before. People asked how much money she made, or mentioned how proud her parents must be of her accomplishments, but never if she was happy. She thought for a moment before answering quietly, "Yeah. I am."

"Then that's all that matters."

"What about you?" she asked.

His gentle smile stole her breath. "I am today, angel."

Chapter Five

Grace and Nick finished their meal in companionable silence. When Nadine asked if they were ready for their check, Grace ordered a piece of apple pie to go.

"Mommy, can I have pie, too?" the little girl at the next booth asked.

The mom sighed. "I'm sorry, baby. I have just enough money for our dinner and gas. If we spend any more, we won't make it to Grandma's."

The little girl nodded solemnly. "That's okay, Mommy. I understand."

Grace glanced at them under her lashes. The mom looked young, no more than twenty, and haggard in a way no one that age should ever be. The little girl had waist-length braids of golden blonde hair and an adorable gap between her front teeth. She was maybe eight. Way too young to understand a budget and not having enough money for a lousy piece of pie. This obviously wasn't the first time she'd had to do without.

Grace's first instinct was to have Nadine send her to-go pie over for the little girl, but something about the mother's tight expression and defeated posture told her charity might not be welcome. Grace made a mental note to pay their tab anonymously when she paid her own on the way out.

"You ready?" Nick asked.

She nodded, reaching for her purse. "I'll take care of the check."

He raised a brow at her. "No, you won't."

Nick made a grab for the check as they stood, but she was faster. "Don't be a Neanderthal," she said. "We're not on a date. I won't let you pay my way."

Nick took a step toward her, then another, until she was forced back against the wall behind their booth. Grace lowered her arms and pressed her palms back against the wall with the check still held loosely between her fingertips as he towered over her.

And he really *towered.* Jesus, had he always been this much taller than her?

She sucked in a sharp breath as he leaned into her and planted a palm on the wall next to her head. Her thoughts scattered until she was left with nothing but the *ohmyGod ohmyGodohmyGod* variety.

His gaze fell to her lips and that was all it took for her body to completely override all common sense. Her nipples leapt to attention as his chest pressed into hers.

And *holy hell* he smelled incredible. If she could bottle that combination of soap and heat and *man*, she'd probably carry it around with her and take hits off it all day like a junkie.

"Grace," he whispered in her ear, sending shivers through her whole body, weakening her knees.

Her answer was a combination moan/sigh, completely unintelligible and completely embarrassing.

"When you're with me, *I pay*."

And with that, he plucked the check from her limp fingers, pushed off the wall and swaggered toward the register.

It took every bit of strength Grace had to not slide down the wall. She glanced over at the young mother who was staring at her open-mouthed, obviously having witnessed the whole show. "Wow," she mouthed.

Grace nodded, still shell-shocked. "I know, right?"

The woman gave her a thumbs-up when Grace found her knees and managed to walk toward the register. "I'd go for it. Good luck, girl," the woman said, shaking her head, looking awed. The little girl giggled. Grace gave her a finger wave.

At the register, Nick was talking to Nadine in low tones. Curious, she sidled up behind him.

"So, you'll send the pie over after we leave?"

"Sure thing, sweetie," Nadine said. "But are you sure you

don't want her to know? I'm sure she'd want to thank you."

Nick visibly grimaced. "God, no." He handed her his credit card. "Go ahead and add her tab to mine, while you're at it. Plus whatever her gas total is."

Nadine finished the transaction and Nick grabbed Grace's to-go bag. He turned on his heel and stopped short when he saw how close she was.

A slight pink tint lit his perfect cheekbones, making Grace realize just how uncomfortable he was to be caught doing something nice for someone. Typical alpha male, she thought. Didn't want anyone to go around thinking he was anything other than a great big jerk.

Then it occurred to her that the balance of power in their relationship had just shifted in her favor. If she wanted to, she could make him regret the little stunt he pulled to snatch the check from her.

But she just couldn't do it. Because the impossible had happened.

Grace had officially developed a crush that wasn't solely physical on her soon-to-be brother-in-law. She hadn't had such mushy, girly feelings since Jaime Lannister battled a bear—one-handed—to save Brienne of Tarth on *Game of Thrones.*

But unlike Jaime Lannister, Nick O'Connor was very real and

about to be related to her. Which made her life more like an episode of *The Jerry Springer* show than *Game of Thrones*. Although, the Lannisters had a decidedly Springer-like relationship themselves, she supposed, so either example would work in her current…

She gave herself a mental pinch. *So not the point.*

"What?" Nick grumbled as she stared up at him.

"Nothing," Grace said as mildly as she could manage, given the circumstances. "That was just a really nice thing to do."

He frowned. "Anyone would've done the same."

She didn't argue the point, but she was pretty sure her ex had never donated so much as a penny to the take-a-penny tray at the Gas-N-Sip.

Nick mumbled something about filling up the Escape and stalked out the door.

"You got yourself a good one there, hon," Nadine said, nodding to Nick's retreating form.

"Well, you're half right," she muttered. "He is a good one."

Too bad he wasn't hers.

Chapter Six

Grace ignored Nick's vehement protests to wait for him to finish pumping their gas before she jogged across the street to get a room at the Sleep Tight motor lodge. She wasn't trying to be contrary, she told herself. She just needed a little space. Some fresh air to clear her head.

But as she stepped into the motel office, Grace instantly regretted her independence.

It wasn't the décor of the office that bothered her. She was, after all, one of a very small group of people who didn't mind '70s décor. Grace thought green shag carpet and gold-flecked Formica counters were funky and retro, and so uncool they were cool again.

What truly freaked Grace out was the leering greeting she received from the motel's night manager, who looked like every serial killer she'd ever seen on *Criminal Minds*.

"How can I help you, beautiful?"

The emphasis he put on "I" and "you" was disturbing, as was his greasy mop of thinning, dishwater-blond hair. He grinned at her, revealing that he had parsley—at least she *hoped* it was parsley—stuck between his two front teeth. Grace suppressed a shudder.

Okay, she told herself. Don't be shallow. So he looks like a deranged mountain man from *Deliverance*. He might be a perfectly nice guy. Give him the benefit of the doubt.

"I just need a couple of rooms for the night," she said.

His gaze fell to her breasts and he licked his lips.

Grace crossed her arms over her chest. So much for the benefit of the doubt.

"Well, now, that can be arranged, little lady." He held out his hand. "I'm Cletus."

She blinked. First of all, no way was she touching this guy. Second of all…Cletus? Really? As in *the slack-jawed yokel*?

Grace held up her hands. "Oh, sorry," she said with a nervous chuckle. "I've been fighting off a cold. I wouldn't want to give you my germs."

His gaze lowered again as he stared at her chest with so much intensity she assumed he was trying to pop her buttons with nothing more than the power of his mind. "I got just the thing to make you feel *good* again," he said.

And she'd just bet it wasn't a cup of herbal tea. *Eeewww.* It was always times like these Grace wished she would've stuck with her Krav Maga class instead of dropping out when she fell and broke her tailbone.

Cletus shoved an old-fashioned register across the desk toward her. "Go ahead and sign in."

Grace signed her name illegibly while standing as far away

from the book as humanly possible. That's when she noticed the pegboard on the wall. There were two sets of keys for every vacant room. A gnawing dread settled into the pit of her stomach. This meant she'd have one set of keys to her room.

And Cletus the slack-jawed yokel—and potential serial killer—would have the other.

Oh. Hell. No.

"So," he said, glancing at the register, then back up at her with a frown, "…beautiful, you said you needed two rooms?"

Her mind raced. What would Penelope Garcia from *Criminal Minds* do?

Oddly enough, that calmed her down. Penelope Garcia wouldn't panic. She'd use her oversized brain and tech savvy to get her out of trouble.

Well, oversized brain she could manage. But tech savvy? Grace could barely figure out how to email someone a picture from her iPhone. Her assistant handled stuff like that for her. What else would Penelope Garcia do?

Inspiration hit like a frying pan upside the head. It was so obvious! Penelope would let one of her hunky FBI cohorts help her.

"Oh, no," Grace said, calmly. "You must've misunderstood. I only need one room." She gestured across the street to where Nick was pumping gas, glaring at her. "That's my boyfriend. He'll be with me." She paused meaningfully. "All night."

So if you were thinking of sneaking into my room tonight, killing me, and wearing my head around like a hat, think again.

"He works for the Department of Homeland Security," she added. *Meaning: he's armed.*

Cletus squinted at Nick, then gave a sad little nod. Obviously he knew when he'd been outclassed. He handed her the key to Room #10 and mumbled something about checkout time the next day before disappearing into the back room, presumably to watch internet porn.

Grace sighed with relief, pretty proud of herself for thinking so quickly in a crisis.

Now all she had to do was spend the night with Nick.

Well, hell.

"So," Nick said, lugging his bag and Grace's two bags into their room. "Why are we sharing a room exactly?"

Because no *way* was Grace planning to jump him, or anything. Nick just wasn't that lucky.

Grace leaned over and lifted a corner of the mattress,

probably looking for bedbugs. He couldn't say he blamed her. He'd slept in some ungodly hell holes in his day, and the thought of those little blood-sucking bastards even gave *him* a screaming case of the willies.

And he certainly didn't mind the view. Grace had a fantastic ass.

She straightened and faced him, blowing a lock of hair off her forehead with a quick puff of air out the corner of her mouth. "Because the night manager looks like every serial killer I ever saw on *Criminal Minds*.

"Is that a show?"

Her eyes widened and she sputtered for a moment before saying, "You've never seen *Criminal Minds*? Do you live under a rock or something?"

He shrugged, tossing the bags on the bed. "I don't have a television."

"You don't have a television," she repeated, incredulous.

"Don't need one."

"What do you do in your spare time?"

"I teach a Brazilian jiu-jitsu class at the YMCA on Tuesdays. I like to run. Read. Go to the movies." He shrugged again. "Whatever."

She shook her head. "Wow. That's unbelievable. I'm not sure what I'd do without *Criminal Minds*. And *Game of Thrones*. And *The Black List*. And *The Walking Dead*."

Now he was incredulous. "You watch all those shows?"

"I work a lot." She lifted a shoulder. "When I'm not working or asleep, I like to watch television. It gives my brain a rest."

Surely someone as gorgeous, smart and sexy as Grace had plenty of friends to go out with and men chasing her. She could have a date every night of the week if she wanted one. He had to assume staying home and watching television instead of going out was her choice. "How long have you been divorced?"

"About six months."

Yeah, that explained it. Probably wasn't ready to date yet. All the more reason he shouldn't be in a hotel room alone with her. Hell, he'd almost pounced on her in the diner, for God's sake. He'd been about two seconds and one more of her hitched breaths away from pinning her to the wall and kissing the hell out of her.

And what really disturbed and excited him in equal measure, was that she hadn't looked like she'd stop him.

He distracted himself by glancing around the room for the first time. "Jesus, it looks like the *Partridge Family* threw up in here."

Grace lifted her hands in a what-the-hell gesture. "You know the *Partridge Family* but haven't heard of *Criminal Minds*?"

He raised a brow. "I didn't say I'd *never* seen television. I just don't have one now."

"Well, let me assure you, programming has improved significantly since the '70s."

"I'll take your word for it," he murmured, glancing around the room again.

He hadn't lied about the décor. It was pure '70s, from the gold foil wallpaper, to the rust-colored shag carpeting, to the orange bedspread with the brightly colored geometric patterns on it. There was even a lava lamp on one of the two chrome and glass nightstands. And since the bed was a double, he imagined he'd be sleeping in the homely little lime-green wing chair in the corner. He sighed. Good thing he didn't usually sleep much.

At least the place was clean. The comforting scent of Pine-Sol filled the air. The housekeeping crew definitely earned their money in this place, Nick decided.

Grace grabbed her carry-on bag and toted it into the bathroom. She came out a moment later with a huge smile on her face. "I shit you not, there's orange vinyl tile in there. It totally reminds me of my Grandma's rec room when I was a kid. I love this place!"

Nick had guessed the moment he saw Grace that if a real,

full-on smile ever graced those pouty lips of hers, the sight would be breathtaking. The kind of smile that lit up a room like sunshine. He now knew he'd been right. Grace was beautiful all the time, but when she smiled…damn.

Something akin to panic grabbed Nick by the balls. In that moment, he wanted her more than he wanted his next breath. A *complicated* woman he'd practically just met. He didn't *do* complicated, and even if he did, she wasn't ready. Not to mention she was way the hell out of his league.

What was the matter with him? First, he'd freaked her out with his intensity, now he was freaking *himself* out. He wasn't used to feeling this many, well, *feelings*.

The smile slowly faded from her eyes. "Nick, are you okay?"

Not even close. "I'm…fine. Just need some air."

And with that, he fled the room like a complete pansy.

Chapter Seven

By the time Nick came back about twenty minutes later, Grace had devoured her apple pie, which was *beyond* fabulous, scrubbed the remnants of make-up from her face, tied her hair up in a messy knot, and was pawing through her bag looking for a nightshirt.

He shut the door behind him, still looking tense, but at least his color had returned.

Grace had no idea what had happened to him, but for a moment, he'd looked like he was going to pass out. If anyone had the right to pass out, it was her. She was the one who had to sleep in a room with sex personified and keep her hands to herself.

Nick pointed at her sternly. "OK, if that night manager gets within fifty feet of you, scream and I'll come running."

She *knew* she wasn't imagining the guy's creep factor. "Hopefully it won't come to that. That *is* the whole point of staying in this room together."

"Yeah, well, at least I now know you aren't prone to exaggeration."

"Did you talk to him?" she asked, still digging through her bag.

He shoved a hand through his hair. "Once he asked me if I

was 'tappin' that hot ass' of yours, the conversation was pretty much over."

"Wow. Complimentary and degrading all at the same time. That's talent." She pulled out her pajama pants, but still couldn't find her shirt. "What did you say to him?"

"Before or after I told him I'd rip his intestines out through his nose if he even *thought* about you again?"

The intensity of his tone caused a little flutter in her stomach, but she ignored it. "Aw, that's so sweet."

His brow furrowed as he watched her systematically destroy the fabulous packing job she'd done in LA. "What are you looking for?"

She threw her hands up in frustration. "I can't find a shirt to sleep in. I don't understand. It was on my list and checked off and everything." She looked back down at her list, where there was clearly a checkmark by *nightshirt.*

Nick tilted his head to one side like a confused retriever. "You have a checklist? For your luggage?"

Great. Like it wasn't bad enough he'd seen her drunk and had to carry her off a plane, now he thought she had OCD. "It helps me make sure I have everything I need before I travel."

He raised that damn annoying brow at her, then glanced at

her ransacked luggage. "How's that working?"

She pursed her lips. "It usually works very well, Dr. Phil. Thanks for asking."

He shook his head, smiling, even though he clearly had no idea who Dr. Phil was. Then he grabbed something from his own duffel bag and tossed it to her. "Here. It will be huge on you, but it should be good enough to sleep in."

Grace caught it and unfolded it. It was a V-neck, heather-gray T-shirt that looked like it had been washed hundreds of times. It was so soft and smelled so heavenly—like Tide laundry detergent and Nick—that she barely resisted the urge to rub it against her cheek and sniff it for a while. Yeah, he was *never* getting this shirt back. "Thanks," she murmured.

He excused himself to take a shower. Grace waited until she heard the shower curtain flip back before changing into Nick's T-shirt and her *SpongeBob* flannel pajama bottoms. She imagined the only way to send a clearer no-sex message would be to wear a sandwich board that said, "No one is getting lucky tonight, pal."

Which was an *entirely* different message than the one her body wanted to send.

She sighed. It was going to be a long night.

***

An hour later, Grace tossed from one side of the bed to the other, somehow managing to wrap the blankets around her tightly enough to cut off the circulation in her legs.

Groaning, she sat up and untangled herself. God, what the hell was the matter with her? It was past midnight, she'd had the longest day of her life, and she couldn't fall asleep.

No matter how hard she tried, she couldn't force her brain to shut down for the night. A million thoughts raced through her head, each one vying for top billing.

First and foremost on her to-do list, she thought as she gave the pillow a good, solid punch, was buying a new nightshirt. Not that Nick's shirt wasn't incredibly comfortable. It just smelled too damn good for her peace of mind.

And then, of course, she had memories of his body against hers as he leaned into her at the restaurant.

God, what had she been thinking? She should have pushed him away. Better yet, she never should have agreed to travel with him in the first place. If she'd just kept a respectable, safe distance she could have gone on pretending she didn't want a man in her life. That she could go on not having sex.

Brad had been a decent husband—at least until he dumped her for Chesty Cheeto—but their sex life had been less than stellar. He'd always been a wham-bam-roll-over-and-fall-asleep kind of guy.

She, on the other hand required quite a bit of warm-up. She tried to talk to Brad about it on a few occasions, and his response was less than satisfying.

"You just need to get out of your head and learn how to relax," he'd said, irritated that she'd even suggested he might benefit from spending some additional time getting to know her clitoris (or even figuring out where it was, for that matter).

After that, she just gave up. Bought a fantastic vibrator with five speeds, which she used once a week. Other than that, her girl parts just went on hiatus. She hadn't even *thought* of sex with someone other than her little battery-operated friend in months.

Until Nick O'Connor.

She groaned out loud and punched the pillow again.

"What the hell is the matter with you?" the object of her sexual frustration grumbled from his position in the chair next to the bed.

Of all the obnoxious… "I'm *so* sorry if my insomnia is disturbing your beauty sleep."

He leaned forward. The soft, muted light from the lava lamp caressed his perfect features and tousled hair. Good grief, he looked like a living, breathing wet dream.

"Not much beauty sleep to be had in this chair."

Thank God, she thought. If he got any more beautiful, she'd burst into spontaneous orgasms every time he walked into the room.

"Are you hungry or something?" he asked, concern evident in his voice.

That's when it occurred to her that she was arguably the most selfish woman in the world. Here he was, spending the night practically folded in half in an uncomfortable chair, for her, a near-stranger.

Grace cleared her throat and sat up. "It occurs to me that I never thanked you."

His dark brows lifted. "For what? For not arresting you? For driving you to River Oak? For spending the night in this chair to protect you from Cletus the potential serial killer?"

"Ugh. Okay, I get it. I'm a horrendous bitch."

"I wouldn't say *horrendous.*"

Even with the only light in the room being supplied by a lava lamp, she could see the teasing twinkle in his eyes. "Thank you, Nick," she whispered.

He blinked slowly and gave her a sleepy smile that would've brought her to her knees had she been standing. She felt as though they'd crossed an invisible border in their relationship.

Which *almost* explained the offer she then extended.

Chapter Eight

Nick had no idea why he'd accepted her offer to share the bed. He could only assume that hearing his name on her lips made him stupid. Okay, stupid*er*.

Grace had fallen asleep almost immediately after he'd gotten settled into bed beside her. Nick, however, remained awake until well after four.

Apparently it was impossible to sleep in a chair next to Grace, and it was impossible to sleep next to her in a bed. At least when he'd been in the chair, he hadn't been aware that she smelled like sun-ripened coconuts and limes. Hadn't been able to feel the heat of her skin. Hadn't itched to brush back the wayward strands of hair that obscured his view of her face.

And for a woman who liked to be in control, Grace didn't exercise a bit of it while sleeping. He'd already scooted to the edge of the bed to escape her flying elbows and knees.

He had to swallow a laugh when Grace muttered a few curses under her breath and rolled to her side. Not even boring in her sleep, he thought wryly.

But any amusement he might have felt died when she tucked her head into his shoulder and threw an arm over his midriff. His entire body stiffened as he watched her, sure she would wake up any moment.

Several minutes passed, and she showed no signs of coming to. Nick relaxed as best he could, considering a gorgeous woman was in his arms, all warm and sleepy.

With a frustrated sigh, he tucked her more fully into the crook of his arm. She responded by inhaling deeply and snuggling closer, drawing one leg up over his to rest her knee just below his groin. And as he struggled to keep his breathing steady, Grace did something she hadn't done all night.

She stayed perfectly still.

Grace sighed as the feel of his warm breath sent tiny shivers of excitement through her entire body. His hand, warm and firm on her breast, had her arching against him, practically begging for more.

In no more than three hot, open-mouthed kisses, he worked her shirt up above her shoulders, giving him full access to her impatient flesh. She felt the heat of his mouth against the hollow at the base of her throat as he cupped her breast, gently tracing his thumb over the distended nipple.

She parted her lips, slowly awakening, yet dreading the moment when he'd slip into the darkness, leaving her with only a hazy dream to cling to. She didn't want to let him go.

"Nick," she whispered.

"Grace."

Wow, best dream ever, she thought hazily. She was almost awake, and yet she could still feel his skin against hers. The scent of soap and laundry detergent and manliness surrounded her. She could feel his rough, strong hands at her waist. Even the shift of the mattress beneath her seemed so very…realistic.

Almost too realistic.

Grace pried one eye open. "Oh," she squeaked, finding herself nose to nose with—and on top of—Nick. It wasn't a dream. He was real, underneath her with his hands around her waist.

And her hand was tucked lovingly into the waistband of his loose cut-off sweats.

"This is either a really good dream, or the beginning of a very awkward-yet-interesting conversation," Nick said, his voice thick with sleep.

"Jesus Christ," she muttered, mortified beyond words, yanking her hand out of his pants. "I molested you in your sleep!" She struggled to roll off him, but her legs weren't cooperating. "I'm a sexual predator. And I'm stuck!"

Grace dropped her forehead to his shoulder. "Why do I keep embarrassing myself in front of you? This has never happened to me with anyone else! Why you?"

His sigh ruffled her hair, sending a shiver that was entirely too pleasant down her spine. “Well, if it makes you feel better, at least you’re not the one tenting the sheet.”

She lifted her head and glanced down at what was indeed an impressive tent. “Oh, wow.” She hoped her tone wasn’t too reverent. It would add insult to injury to let him know how long it had been since she’d been greeted by morning wood.

He obviously misunderstood her tone and rolled his eyes. “Don’t sound so surprised. I’m a guy, and it’s morning. And as if that wasn’t reason enough alone, I woke up with a beautiful woman on top of me and her hand down my pants.”

Her mind raced. Just how far down his pants had her hand been? Had it been wrapped around the hot, hard length now tenting the sheet? Did he realize she’d been dreaming about him while she blindly groped him?

Did he really think she was beautiful?

Focus, damn it, she thought, giving herself a sharp mental slap. He’s going to be your brother-in-law, you shameless slut, she chastised herself. *Stop molesting the man.*

Grace fidgeted again, carefully lifting her hips off his, but she still wasn’t able to put more than an inch between their bodies. “I really am stuck.”

He lifted his head to glance over her shoulder. “It’s the

blankets. They're all tangled around your legs."

When she began to squirm again, he deftly rolled over her and pinned her wrists above her head. "You really need to stop moving," he murmured.

Grace went still, though not because he'd told her to. With Nick's lean, muscled length stretched out on top of her and his mouth only a heartbeat away from her own, she couldn't form a single thought that didn't end with him sliding that impressive erection into her. She simply closed her eyes and struggled to control her ragged, shallow breathing as his hands smoothed their way down over her hips and thighs, untangling the sheets that shackled her to him.

"There," he said after what felt like an eternity. "You're free."

But he made no effort to release her and she made no effort to escape.

"Nick," she whispered, staring up into the depths of his beautiful, unfathomable eyes.

"Grace."

"I'm taking a break from men and dating," she said, the words sounding insincere even to her own ears.

His gaze dropped to her mouth. "I don't get involved with complicated women."

She nodded. "I'm *very* complicated."

"I noticed."

Slowly, as if they had all the time in the world, he lowered his head.

And that's when her phone blared her cousin's ringtone, which just happened to be Disturbed's *Down with the Sickness.*

Note to self: cancel phone service. Immediately.

Nick practically leaped off her in a move so quick and dramatic it would've been comical if she wasn't so turned on.

Grace snatched her iPhone off the nightstand. "What?" she grumbled when she answered.

"Where the fuck are you?" Gage snarled.

"Good morning to you, too, sweetheart."

From his position across the room—Jesus, if he got any farther away from her he'd be in another room—Nick shot her a questioning glance. She lifted her chin in defiance. She didn't owe him any explanations. Let him stew about who her *sweetheart* might be.

"I'm serious, Gracie," Gage said again, sounding incredibly tense. "I need you here. Your mother is trying to set me up with housekeeping."

Grace rolled her eyes. "Do you mean she tried to set you up with *a* housekeeper? You're so dramatic."

"She's tried to set me up with *five* housekeepers in the past two hours," he said through obviously clenched teeth. "That's statistically significant. I'm pretty sure I'm not being dramatic when I say *housekeeping*."

"Well, what do you expect me to do about it?"

"When you're with me, she focuses on you and why you aren't dating, trying to get remarried, or pregnant. When I'm by myself, she's totally focused on *me*."

"And here I thought you might actually miss me. You just want to use me as cannon fodder."

"So? You do it to me all the time."

It was true. She'd often thrown Gage under the proverbial bus a time or two (or ten) to get her mom off her case. She supposed she couldn't fault him for wanting to do the same. "You could always tell her you're gay," she suggested.

She could almost hear him grinding his teeth. "Then she'd just try to set me up with maintenance."

That was true, too. Her mom didn't discriminate. Gay or straight didn't matter. She was an equal-opportunity hopeless romantic who wanted everyone involved in a committed relationship.

"Well, hang in there, you big wuss. I'll be there in…" Grace trailed off, glancing back at Nick.

"If we eat breakfast and get on the road in the next hour," Nick answered, "we'll be there by lunchtime."

Gage must have heard him, because he growled—yes, *growled* like a rabid wolf—in her ear. "Damn it, Grace, are you late because you're holed up in some hotel room having sex with your future brother-in-law?"

She frowned. No way in hell was she explaining herself to Gage, of all people. "Well, when you put it like that, it sounds dirty," she said primly.

"I swear to God, if you don't get here soon, I'm leaving. Grace, I'm not kidding—"

Well, as much fun as the conversation was, Grace was over it. She made a crackling noise in the back of her throat. "What was that, Gage?" *Crackle, crackle, crackle.* "You're…breaking up…can't…hear…need…talk…"

And with that, she disconnected the call and dumped the phone unceremoniously onto the bed next to her.

She glanced back at Nick, who was staring at her, hands on hips, with an expression that said he was about two seconds from darting from the room like Bambi. Oh, boy. This conversation had the potential to be all kinds of awkward. Should she apologize for groping him in his sleep?

But he hadn't seemed to mind, she reminded herself. That much had been obvious, what with the tented sheet and all.

Did he think she was mad at him, or something? Oh, God, he wasn't going to *apologize* to her, was he? Surely he wasn't stupid enough to think he'd taken advantage of her. Or worse yet, that he'd led her on in some way. *Ugh*. That would be beyond humiliating.

He opened his mouth, paused, then closed it with a snap before ducking into the bathroom without a word or a backward glance.

She stared at the closed door in shock for a moment, then rolled her eyes. So they were skipping the awkward conversation and traveling right into the lovely land of denial. Awesome.

If ever there was a clearer illustration of why she was off men, Grace certainly couldn't think of one. There wasn't one of the bastards alive who could communicate worth a damn.

Chapter Nine

Grace had had no idea the landscape in Indiana was so diverse. After what they'd seen on their drive so far, she assumed the entire state was nothing but corn fields and pig farms. But before long, corn fields started morphing into gently rolling hills and lush green woods, complete with fragrant pines and mature oak trees the likes of which Angelenos such as herself could only dream about.

One huge breakfast—Nadine was probably rethinking her all-you-can-eat home fries policy right about now—and an abnormally silent car ride later, Grace and Nick arrived at the resort where they'd spend a week up to their necks in family activities before the big event.

At the end of a tree-lined gravel lane about a mile off the main road, the River Oak Resort and Spa sprawled across what looked like acres and acres of lightly wooded landscape. The structure itself looked to be the love child of an old Southern plantation and the fancy hunting cabin her dad and his old war buddies rented every year during elk season in the Rockies.

The resort's website boasted a par-three golf course, indoor and outdoor swimming pools, horseback riding, and croquet, of all things, in addition to a full-service spa and a small casino. The resort's grounds also had private cabins surrounding the fully stocked lake. All in all, the place had a little something for every kind of guest, including wedding planning services for people who weren't old enough to buy their own beer, apparently.

Nick seemed thrilled to hand the keys over to the valet. She was pretty sure he'd spent the better part of their drive silently cursing the slow-as-Christmas Ford.

God knew he hadn't spent any time talking to *her*.

She was so irritated with him she didn't even protest when he grabbed her bags and his. Telling him she could carry her own luggage would mean talking to him, and if he wasn't talking to her, she'd be damned if she was going to talk to him.

She refused to dwell on how immature that sounded, even in her own head. Or on how easily he toted her bags and his, muscles rippling gracefully with each movement. Bastard.

Grace forced a smile for the older gentleman who held the door for her as she entered the lobby. Nick, right behind her, thanked him. As usual, his voice caused her nipples to perk right up. How the hell did he *do* that?

The desk manager smiled warmly as he checked them in. "I hope you enjoy your stay," he said, then made arrangements for a bellman to deliver their bags to their rooms.

She and Nick mumbled something that sounded vaguely like thanks before going back to studiously ignoring each other.

A shriek sounded from the top of the winding oak staircase,

catching Grace's full attention.

"Nicky!" the woman shouted again, waving her arms like a crazy person fighting off imaginary bats.

Grace turned and glanced at Nick, brows raised, but he didn't notice. He was too busy grinning and moving toward the stairs. Toward the woman.

She was, Grace noticed with no small amount of distress, the kind of woman who inspired loathing and fits of jealous rage in other women. Her hair, which trailed down to the middle of her back in soft glossy waves, was so black it looked blue under the lobby's soft, incandescent lights, and bounced wildly as she moved, making it look like she'd just stepped out of a Pantene commercial.

She looked to be about five-eight, weighing no more than 110. Grace could hate her for that and the hair alone, but there was also the woman's face to consider. It was a perfect oval with nice high cheekbones, a little button nose, and a rosy pair of Angelina Jolie lips.

And she was running toward Nick as if she intended to grab him and never let go. Worse yet, Nick didn't look the least bit appalled by that prospect.

The mystery woman took the last three stairs at once and bounced into Nick's waiting arms. Grace heard a snarl, almost as if a feral cat had been turned loose in the lobby. It took her a moment to realize the ugly sound had come from her own throat.

The woman tightened her grip around Nick's neck. "What took you so long?" she asked. "I thought you'd *never* get here!"

He chuckled and shook her from side to side as he hugged her, earning a little giggle that ended in a snort. Even that little foible was charming.

Okay, this woman had to *go*.

"We ran into some trouble on the road," Nick said, setting her away from him with a playful shove.

"We? Who's we?" she asked in her sweet soprano.

Finally seeming to remember that she was in the room, Nick turned to Grace. "Grace, I'd like you to meet my little sister, Sadie. Sadie, this is Grace. Your future sister-in-law."

And once again, Grace felt like the biggest bitch in the free world.

Sadie turned a huge, warm smile on Grace. "Oh my God. I've heard so much about you, I feel like I know you already."

Air wheezed out of Grace's lungs as Sadie grabbed her and hugged her with a surprising amount of strength for such a willowy girl. Grace's wide eyes flew to Nick pleadingly.

Nick gently pried his sister off Grace. "Let her breathe,

Sadie."

With her space no longer invaded, Grace gave Sadie another once-over. This time, she was more objective, knowing the woman wasn't Nick's friend with benefits or something.

Upon second glance, Sadie was no less enchanting. She shared a perfect olive complexion with her brother, but her eyes were a little bluer than Nick's, less oceanic, more navy. Lovely, nonetheless.

Hell, she looked as if little woodland creatures helped her get dressed every morning. Grace would love to hate her a while longer, but the completely open smile on her face made that difficult. She could totally see why her brother was in love with Sadie.

"I'm glad to meet you," Grace finally said, surprised to find she meant it.

Sadie bounced a little on her heels. "It's so good to finally have someone my age here to talk to about the wedding and everything."

Wow, Grace thought. Either that was the best compliment ever, or Sadie was really clueless enough to believe they were part of the same generation. Meanwhile, standing next to Sadie made Grace feel like an AMC Pacer parked next to a shiny new Lexus.

"I'm happy to help with anything that needs done," Grace offered. *Even if being around you for extended periods of time could be devastating to my self-esteem.*

"Who else is here, Sadie?"

"Well, we purposefully kept the guest list pretty small. It's family only. Michael's here, of course. And his parents, his grandmother, his cousin—though I haven't met him yet…"

Grace resisted the urge to snort. Gage was probably hiding out in his room. The wuss. He was a doctor and Grace was shocked he'd made it through internship into residency, given his general disdain for people.

"…and on our side…" Sadie paused and rolled her eyes. "Aunt Lucille is here."

Nick jerked back. "How the hell did you do that? As far as I know, she hasn't been out of Jersey in thirty years."

"Nickel slots in the casino," Sadie said dryly.

"I guess that'd do it," Nick replied, nodding his head.

"Oh, and there was also one…unexpected guest," Sadie added, shooting Grace what could only be described as an apologetic look.

Before Grace could question her, someone behind her cleared his throat and said, "Hello, Grace, darling."

At that moment, Grace understood what people meant when

they said their blood ran cold—-because she suddenly felt as if she'd just mainlined ice water.

Turning slowly on her heel, she came face-to-face with the last person on the face of the earth she wanted to see. "Hello, Brad," she said quietly.

Chapter Ten

No way had *this* guy been married to Grace.

Had she taken pity on the poor bastard, or was her self-esteem so low she thought she couldn't do better?

Nick wasn't sure which possibility was more disturbing. What he did know, was that doucheBrad had been one lucky SOB.

Brad was about six inches shorter, 50 pounds lighter, and ten years older than Nick. He was also as beige as a guy could get. Plain features, light brown hair and eyes, wire-rimmed glasses, Brooks Brothers suit. He was willing to bet the guy drove a white BMW and the only exercise he ever got was a round of golf at some uppity country club that wouldn't have Nick for a member.

Brad licked his lips nervously and took a step closer to Grace. Nick barely resisted the urge to grab him by the collar of that boring beige suit and toss him out on his boring beige ass.

"Grace, can we speak in private for a moment?"

His voice held a trace of an English accent that even Nick had to admit made him sound smart. Classy, even. It made Nick hate him just a little more. He'd struggled for years to get the Jersey out of his own voice and despite his best efforts, every now and then, it still slipped out.

Grace lifted her chin in a defiant look Nick was quickly

becoming familiar with. He relaxed a little. Grace was going to flay the guy alive. Nick almost wished he had some popcorn so he could sit back and enjoy the show.

"No, Brad, we *cannot* speak privately. I'm here for my brother's wedding. You were not invited. You need to leave."

Sadie cleared her throat. "Well, that's what I told him. But he says your mother invited him. I haven't had time to ask her about it yet, though."

Grace's chin hit her chest and she pinched the bridge of her nose. "Seriously?"

"Quite," Brad said, pushing his glasses up with his index finger. "I let your mother know my intentions, and she was kind enough to invite me to the ceremony and all preliminary activities."

Grace sighed. "What do you want, Brad? What *intentions* could you possibly have for me?"

He brushed an invisible piece of lint off his suit jacket and looked her dead in the eye. "I intend to win you back."

Grace blinked twice, very slowly, before saying, "No, really. What do you want, Brad?"

"Honestly, Grace," he said, sounding a little deflated at her immediate dismissal. "I've realized I never stopped loving you. I want you back."

Come on, Grace, Nick silently urged. *Tell this idiot you wouldn't take his sorry ass back if he was the last guy on the planet. Tell him to get lost.*

Tell him you're here with me.

It was that last part that gave Nick pause.

While Nick stewed silently, wondering what the hell was wrong with him, Grace crossed her arms over her chest and narrowed her eyes on Brad. "Is this about the other woman? Did Chesty Cheeto leave you?"

Brad frowned at her reproachfully. "Don't be crude, Grace. It's not your nature."

Shit, this guy didn't know Grace at all. Anyone who'd been paying attention for more than half a second could see that Grace was passionate as hell, and all passionate people had the potential to be blunt and crude. He shouldn't scold her for it. He should respect and celebrate it.

Just like Nick would've *celebrated* it if Grace's cousin hadn't called and interrupted them that morning.

That thought led his brain down a rabbit hole that could only end with his jeans suddenly becoming too tight. The feel of her—warm and sleepy and soft, on him, then under him—had been as close to perfection as he imagined he'd ever get.

The fact that they'd been interrupted was both a blessing and a curse. On one hand, it was fortunate that cooler heads prevailed and they didn't do something Grace would regret. On the other hand, there was that *amazing* body of hers…

For the second time since they'd met, he'd wanted her more than he'd ever wanted anything, anyone, in his life.

He wasn't used to this kind of emotion. He was an ex-Marine, for God's sake. Marines didn't do a lot of sitting around and discussing their *feelings* with each other. Which was probably why he'd avoided the subject all together and she'd spent the day totally pissed at him. But, hell, he'd rather have her mad at him than thinking he was some kind of obsessed psycho who got too attached too quickly or something.

Grace snorted. "It's *totally* my nature to be crude. You just never realized it because I suppressed it while we were married. I don't suppress *anything* now."

That's my girl, Nick thought.

Wait a minute…no, she's not.

Nick rubbed his temples, suddenly exhausted. Shit, was he really arguing with himself?

Sadie cocked her head to one side and put a hand on his arm. "Nick, you don't look so good. Are you okay?"

Not really, he thought, but nodded. No reason to tell Sadie he was losing his grip on reality.

But then, Brad put his hands on Grace and everything went a little…hazy.

Grace had no clue what the hell was wrong with Brad. The divorce had been his idea, for God's sake. Not that she'd been against it, but still, he'd chosen to leave. Now he was here, at her brother's wedding, showing more passion than he ever had in their marriage? Was she on *Punk'd* or something?

He put his hands on her shoulders and stared down at her, intense in a way she wouldn't have thought him capable before today. "Grace, really. Please believe me. I love you. Our marriage…went off the tracks a bit. But we were good together. You owe it to me—to *us*—to at least discuss reconciliation."

She opened her mouth, but whatever scathing retort she planned to deliver ended in a yelp as a corded forearm snaked around her waist and yanked her back against a solid wall of man.

"That's going to be a problem, Brian," Nick said, his voice very close to Grace's ear.

Brad pushed his glasses up again and narrowed his eyes on Nick. "The name is Brad."

"Whatever. See, I'm afraid Grace won't be giving you another chance. At least, not anytime soon."

"And why is that?"

"Because she's with me."

Grace gulped. Holy fuck! Had *everyone* suddenly lost their grip on reality?

Then Nick pushed her hair over her shoulder and dropped a hot, open-mouthed kiss beneath her ear, and her brain fogged up a bit. Her knees might have given out a little, too. Fortunately, he tightened his grip on her and didn't let her melt into a puddle of lust on the floor at his feet.

Brad's gaze traveled up and down over Nick, then he smirked. "She's with *you*."

Disbelief positively dripped from his tone, and the way he said *you* was just insulting. As if there was *no way* a guy like Nick would be with a woman like her. Like he was totally out of her league, or something. And the fact that Grace thought he might be a tiny bit right just pissed her off even more.

"That's right," Nick said, supremely confident in a way only insanely attractive people could pull off.

"Really?" Sadie squealed. "That's great! Oh my God, Nick, you're going to *love* being a part of this family!"

Well, at least *Sadie* didn't think Nick was too good-looking for her. She practically had them married off. Brad, on the other hand, still looked skeptical.

"This is awfully…sudden, isn't it?" he asked.

Nick's breath brushed across her neck as he curved his body around hers and looked down at her, raising goosebumps all over her flesh. And she really meant *all* over. In fact, Grace had goosebumps in places she didn't even know she could *get* goosebumps.

"Well, Brett—"

"It's *Brad*."

"—when I see something I want, I don't believe in taking it slow."

Nick shifted slightly, placing his hands on her shoulders, and his long, lean fingers splayed over her collarbones. One good deep breath and his fingertips would be on her nipples. Grace leaned back against Nick as she got a little lightheaded at the thought.

Sadie grinned up at Nick, then glanced over at Brad and asked, "So, I guess you'll be going home?"

Brad glared at Nick a moment longer before shifting his attention to Sadie. "Absolutely not. This changes nothing. He is utterly *irrelevant*. This is between me and my wife."

"Ex-wife," Nick and Grace said in stereo.

"A technicality," Brad conceded.

"A *legality*, in fact," Grace muttered. "We both signed the papers."

Everyone ignored her, of course.

"I don't intend to make things easy for you, pal," Nick said, his voice brimming with false congeniality.

Brad's answering smile was far more feral than any Grace had ever seen on him. His voice was pure steel as he said, "I wouldn't have it any other way. I have no doubt the better man will win."

Good grief, Grace thought. *If this goes on any longer, they're likely to whip out their dicks and pee on me right here in the lobby to mark me as their territory.*

That thought and accompanying visual—*ew, gross*!—snapped her back to reality.

Grace turned around and looped her arm through Nick's. "We're done here. Let's go," she said, dragging him toward the elevator. "Sadie, it was a pleasure meeting you. We'll see you at dinner."

Sadie grinned and waved, then turned to Brad and shrugged. "Sorry," she said, sounding sincere. "My brother's a great guy. You probably don't stand a chance. You're welcome to stay for dinner, though."

"Later, Bart," Nick called out over his shoulder as Grace hit the button and shoved him in the elevator.

Chapter Eleven

Grace waited until the elevator doors shut before planting her fists on Nick's chest and shoving hard. It wasn't good for her self-esteem that he barely budged.

Note to self: start strength training program immediately.

"What the hell was that about?" she screeched, dismayed that her voice was a full octave higher than usual. She was sure the shrill sound had dogs all over the state cocking their heads in confusion.

He shoved both hands through his hair, then threw them up in frustration. "Fuck if I know. I just couldn't stand the thought of him putting his hands on you."

She turned her own hands palms-up in the universal what-the-hell gesture. "I was married to the guy, Nick. He's had his hands all over me before." Albeit not very often, and not usually in a mutually satisfying kind of way. But that was hardly the point.

His eyes darkened. "Don't remind me."

Dear God. Was he…jealous? No, that couldn't be it.

But as he started pacing the small space liked a caged wolf, he certainly *looked* jealous.

"Nick, are you *jealous*?" she asked tentatively, fully expecting him to laugh and scoff at the idea.

He stopped pacing abruptly and threw his hands up again. "*Of course* I'm jealous. Isn't it obvious?" The pacing started again. "Oh, and when he got all uppity and insinuated that someone like *you* would never waste your time with someone like *me*? I swear, it was all I could do not to knock his unnaturally white teeth down his stupid British-accent-having throat."

She frowned thoughtfully. "I just assumed he meant that someone like *you* would never be with someone like *me*."

"That's what I said."

True, the words were the same, but the meaning was totally different. Which meant…

"You really *are* jealous," she said, stunned.

"Haven't we established that?" He faced her again. "Jesus, Grace, you're driving me absolutely fucking insane."

Boy, if she had a nickel for every time she'd heard that.

But he went on. "I barely know you, but you haven't left my mind since I threatened to cuff you on that plane."

She blinked up at him. "I feel the same way," she whispered. "But Nick, we're not dating, and I don't want to lie to my family all week."

The heat in his eyes stunned her into taking a step back. He followed, backing her up against the wall and flattening his palms on either side of her head. "Then don't lie. Be with me this week."

The words hit her physically, melting her bones. Fortunately, he leaned into her, holding her up with his weight.

"I don't usually do that kind of thing, Nick."

"I'm not talking about sex," he said quickly.

Well, that was a relief and a huge disappointment all at the same time.

He must have seen the disappointment in her eyes, because his brows raised. "Unless that's what you want." He shook his head, as if clearing it before adding, "But all I'm talking about is spending time with you. As much as possible between now and the wedding."

Oh, boy. This was dangerous territory for her. She was already more attracted to Nick than she'd ever been to another man, even her ex-husband. And to have that kind of attraction to a man she barely knew was absolutely terrifying. "This is crazy," she said. "This morning you could barely force yourself to speak to me."

"Okay, I'll admit it. I was a coward. You terrify me, angel."

She shivered as he brushed a lock of hair off her forehead, his hand lingering against her cheek. "What's different now?" she asked, her voice shaking with what she could only assume was a creamy blend of fear and pent-up lust.

His gaze dipped to her mouth, then back up to her eyes. "I'm tired of being afraid. I want you, Grace. I'll take however much of you you're willing to give me." He rested his forehead against hers. "Just say yes."

She closed her eyes and took a deep breath. "I'm not looking for a relationship, Nick."

He tipped his head to one side, his eyes never leaving hers. "Yeah, but what would you do if you found one?"

Oh, God. That was maybe the scariest, most irresistible thing she'd ever heard. She took a deep breath. "If we do this…"

His head dipped closer to hers and she put a hand on his chest to hold him off. "*If* we do this," she repeated, "it's on my terms. This whole thing"—she gestured between them—"has been crazy and out of control so far. I need more control."

He nodded slowly. "You're in charge. Just say yes."

Her gaze dropped to his mouth. "Yes. But—"

Whatever she was going to say was lost forever as his mouth captured hers.

His lips were warm and firm, yet surprisingly gentle. It wasn't the kind of kiss she would've expected given the hot, hungry look he'd pinned her with, but she felt his desire as surely as she felt her own. He was holding back, she realized, giving her the control she'd asked for.

If she'd been able to think, she would've backed off, put some space between them. But Grace hadn't had sex in a *long* time, and the magic that was Nick O'Connor's mouth had just awakened every girly, lustful part of her body, giving her tingles in places that had never even felt a *twinge* before, so rational thought was a distant memory.

She threaded her fingers through his hair and tugged him closer. Nick growled low in his throat and moved his mouth more deliberately over hers. Grace opened to him and when his tongue touched hers, she thought she'd never tasted anything so amazing in her life. He tasted like peppermint and lust and hot male, and Grace wanted to devour him whole.

He slid his hands down her shoulders, along her ribcage, then slipped his fingertips beneath the snug bottom of her sweater. Hot tingles spread across her chest, her belly, and between her thighs.

But even though he fed her one hot kiss after another, it wasn't enough. She wanted more. She wanted everything—all the passion and fire she'd been missing for so long. She wanted to absorb his heat and feel every inch of his bare skin beneath her greedy fingers.

Grace hitched a leg over Nick's hip and ground against him in an effort to better fit her curves to the hard angles of his body.

She felt his tenuous control snap, felt it in the way his hands tightened reflexively on her ribcage. Felt it in the pounding of his heart against her breast. Felt it in the hard bulge of his…

Wow. He wanted her just as much as she wanted him. The realization played hell with her already-galloping pulse.

And still he wasn't close enough. She needed more. Nick must have sensed her struggle because he slipped his hands to her waist and lifted her. Grace wrapped both legs around his waist in response. She moaned as her hips rubbed against his. A perfect fit.

Panting, he leaned into her, holding her in place with his weight as his hands shifted from her waist to her outer thighs, then up under her so that his hot palms were cupping her bottom.

Grace let her head fall back against the wall as his mouth slid down her neck. She gasped when his tongue dipped into the hollow at the base of her throat. "This is crazy," she whispered as she wound her arms around his neck.

"Uh huh," he murmured against her collarbone. He left one hand on her bottom and used his other to tug down on the V-neck of her sweater. "God, you're so beautiful."

Okay, so maybe this wasn't crazy after all. That was a pretty great compliment, and she couldn't even remember the last time she'd felt so alive. And tingly. There were *definitely* tingles. Hell, her *tingles* had tingles at this point.

He trailed teasing fingertips over the swells of her breasts and her entire body tightened in anticipation. This was only foreplay, she reminded herself, amazed. If foreplay felt like this, could she actually survive sex with this man? Was death by orgasm possible?

She couldn't *wait* to find out.

And just when they'd gone as far as they could with their clothes still on, just when she was on the verge of begging him to drag her to the nearest bed and fuck her senseless…

The elevator dinged and the door opened.

Grace heard a scandalized gasp as Nick slowly lowered her to her feet. She closed her eyes, unable to face, well, *anyone* at this point. Really, how does one hold her head high when she was caught seconds away from screwing a man against an elevator wall?

A squeak escaped her as Nick leaned over and gave the front of her sweater a quick tug up. Her eyes flew open and she found herself reluctantly staring at a wide-eyed elderly couple. The man's eyes were fastened on her breasts, and the woman's eyes were firmly on the front of Nick's pants.

The older woman glanced at Grace. "I miss being young," she said with a wistful sigh.

The man shook his head, eyes still on Grace's chest. "You never looked like *that*, even forty years ago."

She scowled back at him. "Well, you never looked like *him*, either."

Nick grabbed Grace's hand and led her out of the elevator. "Sorry about that, folks," he mumbled.

"You have *nothing* to be sorry about, dear," the woman said, adjusting her glasses as she gazed up at him worshipfully.

"Lucky bastard," the old man muttered as the doors closed.

A hysterical giggle bubbled its way up Grace's throat and spilled past her lips.

Nick glanced down at her, one brow raised. "You think that's funny?"

She shook her head, but couldn't hold the laughter back. Soon, tears were rolling down her cheeks.

Nick grinned down at her. "Grace Emerson Montgomery, you will surely be the death of me."

Chapter Twelve

Grace needed some serious time to think after her encounter with Nick in the elevator, so she slammed her door in his face after promising to talk to him before dinner.

And now, after a nap on truly *fabulous* 600-thread count sheets and a shower in a bathroom fit for a queen, she was finally ready to face the fact that she'd agreed to date her future brother-in-law, even if only for the week. She'd also have to learn to cope with the fact that she'd mauled him in the elevator like a drunken, horny teenager.

One step at a time, Grace. Baby steps.

On a one-to-ten embarrassment scale, this barely rated, right? Certainly not, considering she'd puked on him at 30,000 feet.

Ugh, who was she kidding? This had disaster written all over it. They had so much to talk through before this went any further.

"Nick," she said as she scrunched some frizz-tamer into her hair.

"Yeah?"

Just the sound of his voice in the next room caused a little flutter in her stomach. How pathetic was that?

The fact that they were given adjoining rooms was both a blessing and a curse. With that adjoining door open, as it was now, she could easily carry on a conversation with Nick while they were in their respective bathrooms getting ready for dinner. But with only an open door between them, what would stop her from crossing into his room and finishing their kiss? That amazing, toe-curling, melt-your-clothes-off kiss they'd started in the elevator?

"If we're going to be together this week, I think we should agree to some ground rules."

There was a loaded pause before he said, "There are rules to being together?"

Grace slicked some gloss over her lips. "Absolutely. The first would be that we can't let this get too serious. I meant what I said about not looking for a relationship."

There was another pause before he chuckled, then said, "This must be what people mean when they say karma is a bitch."

Grace frowned at her reflection in the bathroom mirror. "What do you mean?"

"I'm pretty sure I've said that same thing to every girl I've ever dated. This is the first time I've been on the other end of the conversation."

Her heart flipped over. Did that mean he *wanted* more than a casual affair with her? "And that's funny to you?"

"No. Not at all. But you're the boss, Grace. I said I'd take whatever you were willing to give, and I meant it."

That reminded her of her other ground rule, since the things her body was willing to give Nick and the things her heart and head were willing to give him were very different.

"That's the other thing," she said. "Anything…physical that happens with us…I need it to be on my terms."

"I would never pressure you or make you do anything you didn't want to do, Grace," he said, sounding offended.

"I know that," she said, surprised to realize she meant it. Nick wasn't the sort to pressure or cajole her into anything. He was the anti-Brad. "I just want to take it slow."

He laughed, and she conceded, "From here on out."

"That's fair enough," he said. "Whatever you want, angel."

She finished swiping blush over her cheekbones and wandered into his room. "Why do you call me…"

All thought evaporated as she took in the sight of him in front of the bathroom mirror, shaving. Shirtless.

Dear God, there was miles and miles of taut skin stretched over muscles that rippled in places she hadn't known could ripple. And there were—two, four, six—*eight* abdominal muscles visible to her questing eyes. She hadn't even realized that was possible outside of the movie *300* and Photoshop.

He had just the right amount of chest hair, too. Not so much that it looked like he was wearing a sweater (like her uncle Mort), and not so little that rubbing against him would feel like being on a Slip-N-Slide (like Brad). No, Nick's perfect chest had a light dusting of dark hair that narrowed over his abs and arrowed down in a perfect happy trail to his…

He cleared his throat and caught her mortified gaze in the mirror with a knowing one of his own.

Stupid smug Adonis-like man.

"You were going to ask why I call you angel?" he prompted, wiping the remnants of shaving cream from his face with a hand towel.

She nodded, not yet trusting herself to attempt actual words.

He turned and faced her, leaning a hip on the counter and crossing his arms over his chest. The posture was casual, but the heat in his eyes was anything but as he said, "Because I knew as soon as I first saw you that if you ever turned those perfect green eyes in my direction and smiled at me…well, that just might be as close to heaven as I'd ever be able to get." He grinned at her. "And I was right."

And with that, any hope of taking it slow vanished. Without a second thought, she launched herself at him. He caught her easily, swinging her up and around so that she was in front of him, sitting on the counter. Grace grabbed the back of his neck and pulled his mouth down to hers as she wrapped her legs around his waist, locking her ankles behind his back.

Two hours ago—hell, even two *minutes* ago—she would've said there was no way they could ever top the kiss they'd shared in the elevator.

Oh, how wrong she would've been.

This time there was no hesitation, no struggle for self-control. This kiss was all raw passion and hot, blind lust.

After what could have been minutes or hours of tangling tongues and clashing teeth and breathing only each other's air, Grace broke the kiss and rested her forehead on his.

When they both caught their breath, he smiled and pressed a light kiss on the tip of her nose. "I thought we were taking it slow," he whispered.

She gave a wobbly chuckle. "You don't play fair, being all shirtless and hot and saying nice things to me."

His smile widened and his gaze drifted down. "You're not exactly playing fair yourself. You look amazing."

Grace wasn't sure she looked as amazing as the hot look he was pinning her with would suggest, but she *had* put a little extra time into getting ready for dinner.

The full skirt of her favorite red dress fell a few inches above her knee, and the snug-fitting bodice dipped low enough in the front to make the most of her cleavage, yet not low enough to make her look slutty or desperate. The dress was sexy while still managing to be totally classy.

But her mile-high, snakeskin Louboutin ankle boots? Those were pure sex. The epitome of *fuck-me* shoes. This was the first time she'd ever worn them. And she was willing to admit to herself, if not to anyone else, that she'd worn them for Nick. She wanted him to want her as much as she wanted him.

And if the impressive erection pressing into her belly was any indication, she'd succeeded.

Thoughts of his impressive erection quickly derailed her train of thought, forcing her to ask, "What were we talking about?"

His hands slid up her thighs. "I don't remember talking, but I remember *exactly* where we left off."

She giggled—honest to God *giggled*. She couldn't even remember the last time she'd done that. If ever. Had she ever been a giggler?

That gave her pause. Maybe the crazy rush of emotion she felt with Nick wasn't so scary after all. She'd been in control most of her life and she couldn't remember ever giggling. That couldn't be normal, could it? What else had she been missing out on in her life?

"Your thoughts are so loud they're practically hurting my

ears," he said, twirling a lock of her hair around his index finger. "What's going on in that head of yours?"

Her gaze fell to his mouth, just a breath away from her own. "Do you think anyone would miss us if we skipped dinner?"

He sucked in a sharp breath and rested his forehead on hers again. "It would be cruel to tease me about something like that."

She swallowed hard. "I'm not teasing. I'm reconsidering my earlier position on taking it slow."

"Really?"

He couldn't have sounded more shocked than if she'd told him she was a virgin. Frankly, she was a little shocked herself. This was totally out of character for her. She'd only had one lover in her life, and she'd dated Brad for two years before she had sex with him. Now she was ready to jump Nick, who she'd known for about two days.

And somehow, the decision to be with Nick felt more *right* than being with Brad ever had.

She nodded. "Really."

He opened his mouth, but was interrupted by a rather loud, rather embarrassing protest from her stomach. He chuckled. "Something tells me we better not skip dinner."

Grace shrugged sheepishly. "Maybe not. But maybe we can

duck out early instead?"

"Definitely. Are you ready to go?"

She chuckled. "No, no, no. The real question is, are *you* ready to meet my family?"

He raised that sarcastic brow at her. "I don't know. Am I?"

She shook her head and patted his hand sympathetically. "Poor clueless bastard. You'll know soon enough how totally unprepared you are for these people."

He scoffed. "Oh, come on. They can't be that bad."

"Let me leave you with this thought, my friend." She crooked her finger at him until he leaned in so that she could whisper in his ear, "I'm the normal one."

He leaned back and frowned down at her. "Okay, now I'm a little freaked out."

Grace nodded. "Welcome to my world."

Chapter Thirteen

Michael pulled her aside at the entrance of the resort's restaurant, a four-star establishment called Serendipity. Grace introduced Nick and frowned sternly at him when Michael winced as they shook hands. Nick shrugged and winked at her, completely unrepentant.

After brief pleasantries were exchanged (none of which involved threats to disembowel her baby brother if he hurt his sister, thank God), Nick pressed a kiss to Grace's temple and excused himself.

She tried, and failed, to keep her gaze off his butt as he ambled into the restaurant. Really, what the man did for a pair of black dress pants was damn near criminal.

Michael cleared his throat and Grace lifted her guilty gaze to his. "Really, Gracie? You're banging Sadie's brother? Since when? You don't find that a little weird?"

Grace had a pretty good idea that *banging* Nick would be anything but weird. Spine-melting, life-altering, multi-orgasmic, all-kinds-of-awesome *hot*, yes. Weird? No. Complicated, for sure, but never *weird.* "I met him on the flight here. And, no. I don't find it weird. It's not like we're blood relation or anything," she said, repeating Nick's early take on their situation.

Michael frowned at her. "He's going to be our brother-in-law."

Her chin lifted. "Yes, I'm aware. What's your point?"

"Just that it's weird. Incestuous, sorta."

She narrowed her eyes on him and gave him her best dead-eyed lawyer stare. "You know what I find *weird*? The fact that my little brother who's never even had a serious girlfriend before now is getting married." She paused for effect. "*Married.* At nineteen. What's that all about?"

He shifted his weight as he always did when she gave him her lawyerly stare. "Jesus, Gracie," he muttered. "You still talk to me like I'm a kid. I'm a grown-up, damn it."

Grace gave him a good once-over. OK, she'd admit that at a quick glance, he looked like a grown-up. He was, after all, a good nine inches taller than her, and his green eyes sparkled with intelligence. But on the flip side, his sandy blond hair still stood up in the front thanks to the terrible cowlick he'd inherited from their father, and under an ill-fitting suit jacket that looked like it had never met an iron, he wore a white T-shirt with "Suck it, Trebek" printed on it.

Yeah, no way was Michael Montgomery a mature grown-up who was ready to be someone's husband.

"You *are* a kid, Michael," she hissed. "I just don't want to see you make a terrible mistake."

He shook his head, visibly shutting her out. "I'm not talking about this with you."

"What do you mean you're not talking about this with me? You used to talk about everything with me."

"Well, not anymore."

"Okay, ouch," she said, absently putting a hand over her heart. "So now that you're a big adult about to be married you don't need your older sister anymore?"

His lips turned up slightly. "I wouldn't say I don't need you for anything. I was *going* to ask you to be my best man, but now…"

Her jaw dropped. "You were? Oh my God, Michael, that's *huge*."

"So what do you say, Gracie?" he asked sheepishly. "Will you be my best man?"

"Of course I will," she said, grabbing him and pulling him to her for a hug. "I love you, Michael."

"I love you, too, Sis."

And it wasn't until he walked away that she realized he'd totally distracted her from her point, which was that he was too young to get married.

"Damn," she muttered. The slippery little bastard should

have probably considered law school instead of art school.

Good old Brad could take a few lessons in executing a proper stink-eye from Grace's mother.

Sarah Montgomery was a formidable woman, Nick thought. Sure, on the outside she looked harmless with her cloud of soft blond hair that reminded Nick of cotton candy and five-foot-nothing stature. But the look in her blue eyes could only be described as glacial as she eyed the man who stood between Grace and Brad, whom she obviously saw as her best shot at a grandbaby daddy.

What the hell was he doing here? Families always made him feel uncomfortable, like an outsider. Like the orphan he was. He didn't belong here.

But then he thought of his sister's beaming face when he'd seen her earlier and remembered exactly why he was here. He sighed. Damn it. Bailing wasn't an option.

On his left, Grace's stomach growled again. He grabbed the bread basket and shoved it toward her. She smiled gratefully up at him and he felt gut-punched, suddenly knowing he could tolerate anything Brad and Sarah could throw at him if it meant earning even one more of Grace's smiles.

Bailing *definitely* wasn't an option.

"So, Nick," Sarah began, and Nick mentally cringed, thinking, *shit, is it my turn to talk again*? "What is it that you do?"

She didn't say "other than defile my daughter," but it was clearly implied by her tone.

"Jesus, Sarah," Gage muttered. "You know what he does. Why don't you back off?"

At least Gage didn't look at Nick like he was gum stuck to the bottom of his shoe. It was really kind of pathetic how grateful for that Nick was.

Physically, Nick and Gage weren't that different. About six-two, 190 pounds, dark hair, light eyes. That's where their similarities ended, though. Gage was a year younger than Nick and about to finish his residency at Johns Hopkins, which kind of made Nick feel like the not-so-proud owner of the lowest IQ at the table.

He hated feeling that way, too. Nick was proud of his military service and of his current job, but sitting at this table full of white-collar professionals made him feel decidedly unaccomplished. Not that he could let those feelings show. Nick had no doubt Brad would use that weakness against him however and whenever he could.

Sarah placed a splayed hand over her chest and shifted a wounded gaze toward Gage. "What did I do? Am I not allowed to ask questions?"

"I told you what he did before we sat down, Mom," Grace

said, giving her mother a sharp look. "We know you're fishing."

"Like Brad Pitt in *A River Runs Through It*," Gage confirmed, reaching around Nick to snag the bread basket from Grace, who looked like she was considering stabbing his hand with a fork.

If the rest of the family didn't arrive soon so they could start the meal, Nick feared she was going to go all Donner Party on their asses.

Brad, sitting across from Grace, raised a brow. "You can't blame us for being curious, Grace. You show up at a family event with this…man. You can't be surprised that we have questions."

As Nick toyed with the idea of dragging Brad into the men's room and flushing his head in a toilet a few times, Grace swayed forward like a viper preparing to strike.

"You know what, Brad? If I was a good person, I'd tactfully remind you that you lost the right to be curious about my social life when you dumped me for a woman the color of Cheetos whose bra size most likely exceeds her IQ. But I'm obviously not a good person. So I'm just going to remind you that I'm perfectly capable of taking care of myself, and your concern is neither needed nor wanted. You may leave at *any* time if you don't approve of the choices I'm making for myself."

"Hear, hear," Gage said, raising his wine glass.

"Amen to that," Michael muttered, leaning across the table to touch his glass to Gage's.

Brad cleared his throat and adjusted his glasses. "I really don't know how many times you expect me to say I'm sorry, Grace."

"You never said it," Nick muttered.

The bastard had the nerve to look down his smug nose at Nick. "Excuse me?"

"Can't think of one." Gage chuckled as Nick added, "But I *said* that you never apologized to Grace."

"He's right," Grace said. "You said you intended to win me back and that you realized you still loved me. You never said you were sorry."

Brad sputtered for a moment. "Well, I should think that goes without saying."

"Guess it has to in this case, huh?" Michael asked, ripping into a roll.

"Boys," Sarah cut in sharply. "Leave Grace's husband alone."

"Ex-husband," Grace and Nick said in unison.

Sarah ignored them. "I expect that kind of behavior from Gage." She shot a quick glare at Gage, who shrugged. "But I expect more from you, Michael."

"Jesus, Mom," Michael grumbled. "I don't know what you

want me to—"

"Sorry we're late, guys," a sweet voice interrupted.

Sadie practically floated into the room. She looked happier than Nick had ever seen her. His heart pinched at the thought of what she'd gone through—what both of them had gone through—to get to this place in her life.

Sadie wore a scooped-neck dress in a shade of deep blue that perfectly matched her eyes, and her hair hung loose around her shoulders, looking carelessly elegant. The woman in the wheelchair she was pushing in front of her, though? She was anything *but* elegant.

The woman's hair was an odd shade of pale lavender and teased into a short beehive that looked like it was held in place using every pin in the state and possibly some Elmer's glue. If Nick had to guess, he'd say she was about 200 years old.

A man in a tattered cardigan—the kind with leather elbow patches that Nick would've assumed only existed in movies about college professors—wandered in behind them, staring at a Kindle as if it held the secrets of the universe.

Liquid splashed Nick's leg as Gage dropped his glass. Nick grabbed his napkin and started mopping up the mess. Grace grabbed her napkin and began swiping at his pants. "Christ, Gage," she said. "What's the matter with you?"

Nick glanced up and saw exactly what was wrong with Gage. He was staring at Sadie, eyes glazed, mouth slightly agape. He was accustomed to this kind of reaction from men when they first saw Sadie, but it didn't mean he liked it. Nick elbowed Gage sharply in the ribs. "That's my sister," he hissed under his breath.

Gage blinked, but kept his eyes on Sadie.

Grace reached around Nick and swatted Gage on the back of his head. "Michael's fiancée," she clarified sharply.

That did it. Gage gave his head a quick shake, seemingly breaking out of his Sadie-induced stupor.

Introductions were made all around, and Nick learned that the man behind the Kindle was Grace's father, David, and the woman in the wheelchair was her grandmother and David's mother, Ruthie Montgomery.

"O'Connor," Ruthie grumbled, wrinkling her nose.

She looked at Grace over the top of her red-framed glasses and added, "Irish. He'll get drunk and spend all your money."

Grace rolled her eyes. "He has a job, Grandma. He doesn't need my money."

She harrumphed and gave him another once-over, then visually dismissed him. "Good-looking, too. There's no one on earth you should trust less than a good-looking Irishman."

Nick leaned over and whispered to Grace, "She knows I'm sitting right here and can hear her, right?"

Grace shook her head, exasperated. "She knows. She just doesn't care."

"You were better off with that one," Ruthie said, gesturing to Brad.

"Thank you, Mother Montgomery," he cooed with a smarmy smile, making Nick glance around. *There has to be a toilet around here somewhere to flush this fucknut's head in.*

But Brad's smile drooped as Ruthie added, "Better to have a faggot-y Englishman for a husband than a nothing-but-testosterone Irishman."

"Wow," Gage murmured. "You managed to insult gays and everyone in two countries in one sentence. That's impressive, even for you."

Ruthie frowned at him. "No one enjoys your sense of humor."

"I do," Grace said, clinking glasses with her cousin.

"It's no wonder neither of you are married," Ruthie grumbled.

"Grace is married, Mother," Sarah said.

Ruthie's upper lip twisted up into a snarl. "I've asked you

repeatedly not to call me that, you spineless twit."

Sarah smiled and discreetly pushed her bangs off her forehead with her middle finger. "I know," she said sweetly.

"I'm not married," Grace said at the same time Nick said, "She's not married."

"You seem happy, Grandma," Gage said. "Did you run over a puppy on your way here?"

"Grace, Gage," Sarah said, "don't antagonize your grandmother."

"She started it," Grace said defensively.

"She totally did," Gage agreed.

"I don't care who started it, I'm finishing it." Sarah threw her hands up. "I can't believe I just said that to two grown-ups."

"Sorry," they mumbled in unison.

"Besides," Sarah went on, warming to her topic, "this night is about Sadie and Michael. The least you can do is *pretend* you have manners until dinner is over."

"That's not the *least* I could do," Grace said. "I could do *way* less."

"David," Sarah whined. "Speak to your daughter."

David's eyes didn't leave his Kindle as he said, "Poodle, do as your mother says, please."

Nick glanced at Grace. "Poodle?"

She rolled her eyes and said, "Unfortunate perm experience when I was a teenager. Not exactly a story I like to share." He chuckled.

Ruthie leaned back and turned her attention to Sadie. "Are you sure you want to marry into this group of degenerates, dear? I'm sure you're too good for Michael."

"That's no lie," Gage said under his breath.

"Hey," Michael said, sounding like a kid who'd been told he couldn't be Batman when he grew up.

Sadie and Gage locked eyes for a split second before she blushed and looked down at the table.

Grace reached around him to pop Gage on the shoulder. "Snap out of it," she hissed. "She's Michael's fiancée."

"You said that already," he hissed back.

She bared her teeth at him. "I thought it merited repeating."

A waiter arrived and asked if anyone wanted wine. Everyone held their glasses up eagerly.

"Thank you, Jesus," Grace muttered.

Amen and Hallelujah.

Chapter Fourteen

On an average day, Grace knew her family was moderately dysfunctional and quirky. But on a day like today, they were really no better than monkeys at the zoo flinging their crap at one another.

Throughout dinner, her mother continued grilling Nick like she was a detective and he was a perp on *Law and Order*. Her father ignored everyone all night while he read *World War Z*, making Grace regret her decision to buy him a Kindle for his birthday the previous year. Gage's visual fascination with Sadie seemed to border on obsession by the time dessert was served. Michael was especially clueless as he split his time between glaring at Nick and gazing adoringly at Sadie. Nick wore the shell-shocked visage of an avalanche survivor and Grandma Ruthie was…well, Grandma Ruthie.

And now, an hour after dessert with no end to the carnage of the evening in sight, Grace found herself wondering if there was another restaurant in town. Maybe some good old-fashioned comfort food would settle her stomach. The food Sadie had chosen for their dinner left her slightly nauseous. Who the hell chose pumpkin bisque as an after-appetizer soup, anyway?

"Are you okay?" Nick asked.

She was so fascinated with that little furrow in his brow, the one he got when he was concerned about her, that she didn't answer. God, it was so nice to have someone care about her. How pathetic was that?

“You look a little green,” he added, the furrow deepening.

“Maybe the bisque didn’t agree with me,” she admitted.

He nodded. “Not surprising. It looked like baby crap.” He gestured for the waiter and asked him for a bottle of water.

The fact that it looked like crap was probably what kept the men, other than Brad, from eating any of the bisque. Smart. Her stomach roiled and she groaned. If only she’d been smart and avoided it, too.

“It gave me gas,” Ruthie said, then underscored her comment with a loud belch, not bothering to cover her mouth.

“Lovely,” Gage muttered.

Sarah dabbed at her sweaty forehead with a napkin. “I guess that wasn’t a good suggestion after all. I’m so sorry, Sadie, dear.”

Grace silently took back the nasty things she’d been thinking about Sadie’s choice in food. She should’ve known that the pumpkin bisque had been her mother’s idea.

Sadie smiled weakly, still beautiful, even though her alabaster skin had turned pasty and clammy-looking. “That’s all right. I still appreciate your help. I didn’t have any clue what to order.”

The waiter arrived with Nick’s water. He accepted it with a

nod of thanks, then twisted the cap off and handed it to Grace. "Drink this. I wasn't about to let them bring you tap water. I don't even trust *that* after the bisque fiasco."

He said *bisque* with the same enthusiasm she showed for big hairy spiders. Grace smiled up at him. He smiled back and they kind of…stuck like that. The noise around her dimmed and her stomach calmed for a moment as she focused on his face. Those amazing eyes with the little smile lines at the corners. And Jesus, who knew men could even have lashes that thick?

"Angel," he said, voice pitched even lower than usual. "If you don't stop looking at me like that, I'm carrying you back to your room caveman-style and pinning you to the wall for a few hours."

Her breath whooshed out. That sounded *way* better than it probably should have.

With a growl he leaned toward her.

Brad slammed his fist down on the table, sending the bread basket and his wine glass flying. "I've had just about enough of this," he shouted.

Grace and Sadie jumped, but Nick calmly shifted his gaze from Grace to Brad, raising a brow expectantly.

"Grace, I've tolerated this charade long enough," Brad said.

"Great leapin' horny toads," Ruthie muttered, mopping up

the spilled wine with a handkerchief she'd pulled from her bra. "I guess the little fairy has a backbone after all."

Sarah wrung her hands anxiously. "Brad, maybe you should wait—"

He gave his head a furious shake. "No. I absolutely *will not* wait another moment to tell Grace how I feel."

"Sweet Christ," Gage grumbled, downing what remained of his wine. "What a clusterfuck."

"Brad," Grace said with a sigh that felt like it came from her toes. That was how deeply exasperated she was with Brad at the moment. "Can't we talk about this in private? Tomorrow, maybe?"

He slammed his palms down on the table again and leaned forward. "And let you spend the night with this piece of…" He gestured to Nick, his lip curled up in disgust, "…trailer trash? I bet he didn't even bother telling you he's the son of a drug dealer who died in a prison brawl."

Nick's eyes narrowed, and every bit of color drained from Sadie's face. Everyone else at the table went deathly quiet.

Michael looked at Sadie, whose lower lip began to tremble. He frowned. "But I thought your parents died in a car accident."

Sadie's mouth opened and closed like a landed trout, but no sound came out.

"No," Brad went on, clueless as ever, pointing an accusatory finger at Nick, "they didn't. His mother was stabbed to death in prison while serving time for dealing. His father died of an overdose while awaiting trial, also for trafficking."

Nick ignored him and shook his head at Sadie. "I'm so sorry, honey."

Michael looked at her like he'd never seen her before. "You lied to me?" he whispered. "Why?"

Grace knew the mulish look on Michael's face. She'd seen it a million times over the years. If she let him dig his heels in, the marriage would be off, which was exactly what she wanted. They were too young to get married, anyway. All she had to do was keep her mouth shut and the problem would go away.

But one look at Sadie's distraught face and she knew she couldn't let it go down like this.

"Well, just wait a minute, Michael" Grace said calmly. "This is probably just a crazy misunderstanding. Brad, where did you get your information? Did you run a background check or something? And more importantly, why would you purposefully try to hurt Sadie like this?"

Every drop of righteous indignation bled from Brad's face as comprehension final sank in. "Their aunt told me," he murmured. "I met her in the casino." He gulped. "Miss O'Connor, I-I never meant to hurt *you*, I swear it."

"No, you were so damn busy trying to hurt her brother you never once thought about her feelings," Gage said with a disgusted sneer. "You always were a sniveling little shit, but this is low even for you."

"Why would you lie to me, Sadie?" Michael repeated, sounding more than a little hurt and pissed off.

Sadie just shook her head, tears filling her eyes.

Nick ran a hand through his hair. "Jesus, wouldn't *you* lie? What this little douchebag dug up? That's not even half of what they did. She's ashamed of them. I would be, too, if I gave a shit."

But he did, Grace realized. She could see it in the tight set of his jaw. He just hid it better than Sadie. Her heart broke for these two obviously good people who were ashamed of their upbringing, of who they were.

Grace cleared her throat, trying to get rid of the lump that had settled there. "Well, Michael, let's talk through this." Because if there was a single thing in this world Grace Montgomery was good at, it was mediation. Law school had seen to that. "Can you honestly tell me that *you* haven't lied to Sadie about anything over the course of your relationship?"

His chin came up defensively. "I haven't lied about anything."

Mistake number one, she thought. Never give a lawyer an absolute. "Nothing at all? So, you told her about how you wet the bed until you were ten?"

Michael's outraged intake of air practically sucked all the oxygen out of the room. "You promised you'd never mention that!"

She smirked. "I lied."

He sputtered for a moment before regaining his composure. "Well, it wasn't technically a lie. I just didn't mention it."

Mistake number two. Don't argue technicalities with a lawyer. "It was a purposeful omission, which, if we were in court, I would argue was a lie."

She'd *argue* it. Couldn't make it ever stand up in court. But Michael didn't need to know that.

Sarah threw her napkin down. "Grace Emerson Montgomery, you apologize to your brother. Bringing up his little…problem was uncalled for."

"Just trying to prove a point, Mom." And take the heat off Sadie, of course. "We all have things we're ashamed of and might lie about if given the opportunity."

Michael crossed his arms over his chest. "Yeah, like when you were thirteen? When you said you were spending the weekend at Sheila McElroy's house?"

Grace narrowed her eyes at him. "You wouldn't."

He smirked. "She was really at a Bon Jovi concert with Sheila's brother. Sheila's *eighteen-year-old* brother."

Sarah gasped. "Damn it, Grace, you could've been raped or killed or…" she trailed off and pointed a finger at Grace, "you're grounded."

"I'm twenty-seven years old and live in a different state. You can't ground me."

Sarah pursed her lips. "David, say something."

He didn't lift his eyes from his Kindle, but parroted, "You're grounded."

Ruthie cackled, then belched loudly without bothering to cover her mouth—again. She pounded her chest lightly with her fist twice before saying, "Whoa, Nelly. That bisque was a pip, wasn't it?"

"Fine," Grace said, "I'm grounded." She rolled her eyes. "My point is that we all have secrets, things we're ashamed of and don't want to tell anyone about. Like Brad, for example."

Brad sputtered. "I don't really see how that's relevant at all to—"

"He wears lifts in his shoes," she said, looking down her nose at him. "He's really only about five-six."

Sadie's lip finally stopped trembling and her eyes brightened a bit. Gage must have noticed because he admitted with a careless shrug, "I have a juvenile record."

Grace nodded. "He stole a car when he was twelve."

"Borrowed," he corrected.

"Nuance."

"You were a complete turd," David said, still sounding distracted and not looking up from his Kindle.

"Thanks, Uncle David."

He grunted in reply. Sarah buried her head in her hands as she cried, "I don't think I've ever been more ashamed of you children."

Grace narrowed her eyes. "What about you, Mom? I know you're not perfect, either. What secrets are you hiding?"

Her head shot up and her eyes went deer-in-headlights wide. "Nothing," she said too quickly.

Gage raised a brow. "Uncle David?"

Her father lifted his head and blinked a few times before saying, "She smoked pot in the late '70s and early '80s. A lot of it." He gave Sadie a wink before returning his attention to the zombie apocalypse.

Her mother let out a shocked gasp, threw down her napkin, and jerked to her feet. "I've had just about enough of this. I'm not feeling well and I'm going to bed."

As she turned on her heel and strode from the room, head held high and regal, Gage turned to Sadie and said, "Can't help but notice she didn't deny it."

Sadie giggled, then slapped a hand over her mouth as if she couldn't believe such a sound had come out of her. Gage graced her with one of his rare smiles that—Grace had been told—could stop a girl's heart...or drop her panties. Sadie didn't appear to be immune, as red stained her cheeks and she dropped her gaze to the table.

Grace's stomach rumbled ominously, letting her know it was time to cut the evening short. "Look, it's been a long night. Michael, why don't we all go our separate ways so you and Sadie can talk privately?"

Everyone got up and mumbled their goodbyes. Grace noticed that her brother left the table and didn't look back at Sadie once. Gage noticed, too.

"That fucker," he muttered. "No way could the golden boy understand what she's going through."

Grace hated it when Gage called Michael that. It wasn't Michael's fault that her parents doted on him. Or that Gage's parents were neglectful shitheads who completely abandoned their son and disappeared when he was just a kid. "Let it go, Gage. Michael will come around."

He grunted in reply before adding, "Hey, nice job sticking up for her tonight."

He held out his clenched fist and she rolled her eyes as she bumped knuckles with him. "What are you—twelve?"

He flipped her off and headed to the elevator. She glanced back at Nick, who was watching her with the most intense expression she'd ever seen directed at her.

And God knew that as a lawyer, she'd had some pretty damned intense expressions aimed at her a time or two.

"What is it?" she asked warily.

He didn't answer. Instead, he grabbed her hand and tugged her into an elevator. When the doors closed, he shoved her against the wall and captured her squeak of surprise with his mouth.

When she was pretty sure he'd melted every bone in her body with the passion and heat in that kiss, he rested his forehead on hers and said, "You're amazing, Grace Montgomery."

"Huh?" she asked, dismayed that eloquence had completely escaped her.

"I know you're against my sister marrying your brother, and when you had your shot, you didn't take it."

Grace sighed. "I'm not against your sister at all. I'm against a couple of children getting married. But still, your sister seems great. I didn't want to see her get hurt like that. She doesn't deserve it."

He pushed a curl behind her ear, letting his fingertips linger on her skin. "That's why you're amazing. No one but me has ever stood up for Sadie before."

"Well, that's just…not right." She frowned. Apparently her eloquence was still MIA. Or maybe she'd never had any with Nick to begin with.

He smiled and leaned in for another kiss. She braced herself against the wall, just in case her knees gave out. Again.

But just as his lips were a whisper away from her own, the elevator door opened and a harried-looking Gage stepped inside. "Thank God I found you. How are you feeling?"

Annoyed? Sexually frustrated? Damn tired of getting interrupted? Take your pick, she wanted to say.

But she didn't say any of that. Instead, she turned to Nick, opened her mouth, and for the second time in their short acquaintance…

She threw up all over his shoes.

Chapter Fifteen

"I have *Ebola*."

Nick shook his head and pushed her hair off her sweaty forehead as she rested her cheek on the toilet seat. He was pretty sure she'd just heaved up more food than he'd eaten all week. No doubt she *felt* like she had *Ebola*. Hell, his stomach hurt just *watching* her. "Gage was pretty sure it's food poisoning. Unless you, your mom, Sadie, and doucheBrad all have Ebola."

She groaned and curled into the fetal position on the bathroom floor. He wished he could carry her to bed, but every time he'd tried, the movement made her puke again. So, he settled for gently shifting her so that his thigh was between her face and the cold marble tile.

"I'd be so embarrassed if I wasn't dying," she muttered.

Feeling completely helpless and hating every minute of it, he laid a cool, damp washcloth across her forehead and smoothed her hair behind her ears. "I've told you before that you've got nothing to be embarrassed about with me, angel."

She snorted, then moaned. "I've puked on you. Twice. You've seen me with my head in the toilet. A lot. There's not a woman alive who'd want to be seen by a man who looks like *you* when she's like *this*."

"Tell you what. Next time I have the flu or food poisoning,

I'll give you a call so you can see me with my head in the toilet. Then we'll be even. How's that?"

"That'll work."

"Good." He lifted her clammy hand and kissed her fingertips. "No more being embarrassed with me."

She struggled for a moment to lift her head before letting it drop back to his thigh. "Yeah, about that," she said with a frustrated sigh. "I could use some help changing my clothes."

Under normal circumstances, he might've made a joke about her request to help get her out of her dress. But at the moment, he just wasn't in a laughing mood. "Sure. Want the T-shirt you slept in last night?"

"That'd be good," she said against his thigh.

"Ready for me to try and move you again?"

Grace blew out a sharp breath. "Oh, sure. Why not? I mean, it's been, what, three minutes since I last vomited?"

"I'll be extra gentle."

"Do you really think you can dead-lift me off the floor?"

In answer to her question, he lifted her straight off the floor without even really trying and climbed as slowly as possible to his feet. Her head lolled against his shoulder and she gave him a weak smile that pinched at his heart.

"Wow," she said. "That would've been really sexy if I hadn't just been on the bathroom floor."

"We'll try it again when you're back up to a hundred percent."

He laid her on the bed and she rolled to her side so that he could unzip her dress. He refused to notice the miles and miles of smooth skin and lacey red underwear exposed as the zipper made its long, slow, torturous journey down. Refused.

Through some miracle, he managed to shimmy the dress off her pliant body and slip the T-shirt over her head. She shivered. "Cold?" he asked.

She nodded, teeth chattering.

He crawled into bed and sat back against the headboard before easing her up so that she sat between his splayed legs with her head on his chest. She burrowed into him when he tucked the blanket around her.

"You're so warm," she murmured.

Yep. On fire. Had been since he first met her.

Her phone buzzed on the nightstand, and he saw that it was Gage, so he answered for her.

"How's the patient?" Gage asked.

"A little better, I think. She hasn't puked in like, what, five minutes?"

Grace groaned against his chest. "Don't say 'puked.'"

He chuckled and kissed the top of her head. "Sorry. Gage, how's my sister doing?"

"About like Grace, from the sound of it."

Grace looked up and whispered, "If you need to go be with Sadie, I understand. I'll be OK."

Nick frowned down at her. She was so weak she could barely move, and she was giving him permission to leave. There was selfless, and then there was just martyrdom. Grace was currently within kissing distance of the latter. "I'm staying." To Gage he said, "Michael is with Sadie, right?"

Gage snorted. "Yeah, right. He saw her puke once and ran for the hills. I'm with her, though. I won't leave her."

Nick heard weak protests in the background, then Gage's muffled response: "Okay. I'll tell you what. If you can stand up on your own and walk to the bathroom by yourself without hanging onto the furniture, I'll leave."

A moment of silence, then Gage said, "Yeah. That's what I thought. Like I said, I'm not leaving."

Nick sighed. "Grace, honey, would you feel better if we switched and Gage stayed with you and I stayed with Sadie?"

She shook her head and burrowed into him deeper. "Nope. I'm warm."

Gage must have heard, because he said, "I'd rather stay with Sadie. She's underweight and already dehydrated, so she needs someone with her who'll push her to drink at regular intervals. I'm more likely to do that than you are. Especially since I seem to bring out her cantankerous side."

Nick heard his sister's muffled voice again before Gage told her, "Yep. That's right. He's a nice guy and I'm not. Michael's a nice guy, too. But I have one advantage over them: I'm here."

Good point, Nick thought. Harsh, but good.

It didn't sit well with Nick that Michael didn't stick around and take care of Sadie. Even if he was mad at her for not telling him the truth about their family, it seemed like the least he could do was hold her hair back for her while she puked.

And knowing Sadie, she'd never ask him to. The kid had never asked for anything her whole life.

"How're my mom and Grandma Ruthie?"

Nick opened his mouth to direct Grace's question to Gage, but he must've heard her, because he answered, "Your mom is sleeping. Your dad put his Kindle down long enough to take care of her. And Ruthie never got that sick. Just a mild case of indigestion."

"How is that possible?" Grace asked. "I saw her eat the bisque. I think she even ate more than I did."

Nick practically heard Gage shrug. "She's immune, I guess. More proof that she is, in fact, the devil. I'm only worried about you and Sadie at this point. With her weight and your crazy metabolism, you two are in the most danger."

"What about Brad?" Grace asked.

Nick frowned. Food poisoning was too good for that son of a bitch.

"Like I said, I'm only worried about you and Sadie at this point," Gage said dryly.

Grace sighed. "Will you check on him, Gage?"

"No. But I'll send your dad to turn him over if he's face-down in his own vomit. Good enough?"

Nick felt Grace smile weakly against his chest. "Good enough."

"What do I need to do for her, Gage?" Nick asked.

"Keep her hydrated. Just little sips of water often until she can hold it down. After a few hours of that, she can drink as much as she wants, but I want her to lay off food for a while. We'll start her on dry toast and bananas tomorrow."

"You sound like you're talking about an infant," Grace said on a groan. "Should he burp me and change me while he's at it?"

Nick chuckled, then thanked Gage and ended the call.

"Think you can rest a little now?" he asked.

She snuggled in closer, her hip pressing against his groin, and he barely suppressed a groan.

"I don't think so," she said. "Want to watch some TV with me?"

He hated TV. But he'd pretty much give her anything she wanted at this point if it made her happy. At least this was something he could *do* for her. "Sure."

Chapter Sixteen

"Jesus, I thought they were brother and sister!"

Grace smiled as Nick sat up straighter, as entranced by the show as she knew he'd be. Even people who didn't normally watch television—which just seemed un-American to Grace—couldn't resist *Game of Thrones*. Wait until he saw what Jaime Lannister was going to do to—

"Holy fuck! Did he just push that kid out the window?"

"Yep."

Nick lapsed into speechlessness as the final credits rolled, which Grace understood completely. The show had done that to her more times than she could count.

Grace snagged the remote out of his hand and shut off the television. He let out a disappointed sigh and asked, "Ready to get some rest?"

"No," she said. "I just need to rest my eyes. Keep talking to me."

And he did. They talked for hours.

They covered everything from his days as a poor trailer park kid in Jersey, to his time in the military, to the attack that ended his career as a Marine, opening the door to his career as an air marshal.

They talked about her awkward preteen years, before she found make-up and a good hair gel to tame her unruly mop of hair, back when she wore glasses *and* braces *and* was sure no one would ever love her.

He listened intently as she talked about her marriage, and her guilt for not feeling, well, *more* about its demise.

Then, because the conversation was getting way too heavy for her liking, she switched to lighter fare.

“Iron Man or Batman?”

He scoffed. “Duh. Superman.”

Typical dude answer. “Wrong. The correct answer is Iron Man. Although, you could’ve made an argument for Batman. Superman is just wrong.”

“Self-centered rich dudes with God complexes over an alien superhero?” She felt him shake his head. “It’s not even close. Besides, I thought you’d choose Wonder Woman.”

Now she scoffed. “No way. That invisible jet thing is just lame. Ruins her whole image.”

“Fair enough. John McClane or Martin Riggs?” he asked.

This time she scoffed. “Jason Bourne.”

He chuckled. “Touché. *Star Wars* or *Star Trek*?”

"Trick question. Both are right. Unless you're talking about the *Star Wars* prequels, then I say nuke Anakin. And if you're talking about *Star Trek: The Next Generation*, I say nuke Wesley."

"OK." His fingers found their way into her hair and gently started shifting through the strands. Grace fought the urge to rub against his hand and purr like a kitten. "Football or baseball?" he asked.

"MMA fighting."

"*You* like MMA fighting?"

"Don't sound so surprised. Just because I'm a girl doesn't mean I can't enjoy two burly dudes beating the crap out of each other. And it takes more skill and stamina than football and baseball combined."

"True enough. Music?"

"Anything but country."

He held up his hand for a high-five, and she slapped her palm to his. Nick smiled. "See?" he asked. "We were destined to spend this week together. We're practically soul mates."

Her heart seized. It really wasn't fair for someone like him to say that to a semi-bitter divorcée such as herself. It did unspeakable things to her ovaries.

He sighed. "Don't overthink it, Grace."

"What?"

"I can practically hear the gears in that giant brain of yours locking up," he said. "I'm not going to push you into anything you're not ready for. Just enjoy the moment."

She snorted.

"Okay," he conceded. "Maybe not this *exact* moment. But when you're better, just…go with the flow a little. Let things happen on their own."

The words sounded foreign to her. She was a born planner, a strategist. She could come up with a plan for how to *plan* more efficiently, for God's sake. Enjoying the moment was not something she had much experience with.

But then again, she had even less experience with guys like Nick and the way he made her feel. "Fair enough," she finally whispered.

He pressed his warm lips lightly against her temple. She shivered in response. "Get some sleep, angel. You'll feel better in the morning."

She sure hoped so. Because right now, she was starting to feel like maybe the food poisoning wasn't such a terrible price to pay for the privilege of falling asleep in Nick O'Connor's arms.

And damned if that didn't make her feel like a heroine in one of the old Hallmark Channel movies she used to mock with Gage.

Grace Montgomery: pathetic is thy name.

Chapter Seventeen

Nick had lost all feeling in his arm and one leg hours ago, and he had a crick in his neck that he would surely be feeling for days, but he could honestly say, he'd slept better than he had in…well, *ever* he supposed.

For the first time since his discharge from the Marines, Nick slept the kind of sleep he assumed normal people—people who hadn't almost been turned into chum by an IED—slept every night. Blissful, sound, dreamless sleep.

He supposed it could be because he was starting to move past the trauma, starting to heal both physically and mentally. But in the back of his mind, he couldn't help but think his peaceful sleep had nothing to do with healing and everything to do with the soft, warm woman lying so trustingly in his arms.

Grace was sprawled on top of him with her head on his chest and her tousled hair splayed over his shoulder and throat. One of her arms was flung over his stomach, and her knee was tucked up snugly against his groin.

Even after the night she'd had, her hair still smelled faintly of limes and coconuts—a scent he realized he would associate with Grace from this point forward. And like Pavlov's freakin' dog, the scent would probably always make his mouth water, like it was now.

Grace let out a snuffling little snore and tucked her hand into the waistband of his pants. He groaned, torn between amusement and arousal. Seemed Grace was a bit of a slutty sleeper.

Too bad for him that sluttiness didn't carry forward into her waking hours.

When Grace roused and yanked her hand out of his pants, muttering a horrified curse under her breath, Nick pretended to be just waking up himself to spare her the embarrassment of being caught molesting him two mornings in a row.

Grace eased off him, then groaned and flopped over on her stomach next to him.

"How are you feeling?" he asked quietly. "Any better?"

She turned her face toward him, but didn't lift her head off the bed. "Well, I don't think I'm going to die anymore."

He grinned as he took in her wildly tousled—and completely vertical in random spots—hair and the thick mascara smudges under her eyes. Even though her skin was unnaturally pale and she looked like she'd been wrestling with a cougar half the night, she was gorgeous.

"It's nice of you to pretend you were asleep while I was molesting you," she added.

So much for trying to preserve her dignity. "I was just afraid you'd stop if I moved or said anything."

She snorted with laughter, then moaned and pressed her hand to her forehead. "Oh, maybe I spoke too soon about that whole not-dying thing."

"Headache?"

"Yeah."

Nick stood up and rolled his neck from one side to the other, then gave his arms a shake, willing the blood to start flowing through them instead of pooling uselessly in his groin. When he could feel his hands again, he grabbed Grace a couple of aspirins from his overnight bag.

He twisted the cap off a water bottle and handed it to her, along with the aspirins. "Gage said last night that if you kept some water down, I could give you these if you needed them. Then, if those stay down, we can start on food."

She grumbled, but took the aspirins. "I don't think I'll ever be able to eat again."

He sat back down on the edge of the bed and brushed her hair back off her forehead. "Yeah, I had food poisoning once and thought the same thing. You'll be back to normal by tomorrow. You're tough, Grace Montgomery."

She blinked up at him. "I am?"

"Had to be to survive dinner last night. And I'm not talking about the bisque."

She laughed outright this time. "That was typical. Nothing special at all."

He couldn't stop his gaze from dropping to her mouth, and he heard her breath catch. "No, that's where you're wrong," he said, his voice even lower and rougher than usual. "There's nothing typical about you, Grace."

Chapter Eighteen

It was actually three days before Grace felt well enough to venture out into the world.

Guess she wasn't as tough as Nick thought she was.

But despite it all—the vomiting, the endless binge watching on Netflix, which she knew he hated, being stuck in bed, her being practically tethered to the toilet—Nick never left her side.

They'd only known each other a few days, and yet, she felt closer to Nick than she could remember ever feeling to Brad—or any other man in her life, for that matter. She knew it was insane. There was no such thing as love at first sight. And yet…

He'd taken care of her time and time again. He could've left her with Gage, or let her parents take care of her. But he'd stuck with her for days in a room that smelled like stale air and vomit, talked to her, kept her company, made her laugh and feel desirable, even when she knew she was hell and gone from looking her best. And then there was the way he looked at her.

Nick looked at her like she was priceless. The most incredible thing he'd ever seen. No one had ever looked at her like that. No one.

She'd even gotten over her embarrassment at waking up draped over him every morning. It seemed her body just took whatever it wanted during the night.

Every night, she went to sleep on her side of the bed. And every morning, she woke up in the same position: splayed across Nick's chest with her face buried in the crook of his neck.

There was always a moment before she was fully awake, before her brain told her she should pull away from him, when she was just able to *feel.* Feel safe and warm in his arms. Feel turned on by the slide of his warm skin against hers. Feel the possessive way that, even in his sleep, he cupped the back of her head in one hand, and her ass in the other.

It was her favorite part of the day.

Her favorite part of the night? Well, that was entirely different. And much dirtier.

Her brain had treated her to countless wet dreams over the past few days. All X-rated, all starring Nick. The one that kept recurring was Nick in the shower, water sluicing over miles and miles of tanned muscles as she fell to her knees in front of him and wrapped her lips around the long, smooth length of his…

"Grace, honey, are you feeling OK? You're all flushed and sweaty-looking."

Her mother's voice was the equivalent of face-planting into a snow drift, reminding her that she was in Sadie's room and shouldn't really be having sexual fantasies about Nick while the poor kid tried on her wedding dress. Her body instantly chilled back to its normal temperature. “I’m fine, Mom.”

If only her panties were as dry as her tone, she thought wryly.

“She’s thinking about that Irishman,” Grandma Ruthie said. She pulled a tissue out of her bra and honked into it. “I can tell by the stupid smile on her face.”

Her mother looked nervous. “Grace, I’m not sure I like this O’Connor boy,” she said quietly, presumably so that Sadie, who was trying on her wedding dress in the bathroom, couldn’t hear.

Grace snorted. Nick O’Connor was as far from a *boy* as she’d ever been with in her life. He was *all* man. “He’s a good man, Mom. Leave him alone.”

“You barely know anything about him.”

She raised a brow. “I know more about him than you do. So, who are you to judge?”

“I never should’ve sent you to law school,” her mother grumbled. “You’re always so argumentative.”

Ruthie stuffed the used tissue back into her bra. “He probably goes through your purse every night while you sleep. I told you that you can’t trust an Irishman. You’ll see. All sperm, no scruples.”

Grace zoned out again as her mom and Ruthie argued about…something. She didn’t really care to listen or get involved.

She straightened up in her chair when Sadie stepped out of the bathroom, biting her lip, looking hesitant.

Sadie turned a small circle, arms held wide. "Well, what do you all think?"

Sarah clasped her hands in front of her as her eyes filled with tears. "Oh, honey, you look lovely. Just lovely."

Even Ruthie murmured her agreement.

Grace frowned. "Mom, is that your old wedding dress?"

Sadie's anxious eyes rose to Grace's. "You don't mind, do you? I just had trouble deciding on what I wanted to wear, and your mother offered me her dress."

"No, of course I don't mind," Grace was quick to add. She'd been offered the same dress when she married Brad. She just hadn't worn it because it was so far from her usual style.

There was no denying that Sadie looked like an angel—or, an underwear model dressed up like an angel—in the vintage dress. The delicate lace draped over her perfect form like it was made for her. But the style was so old-fashioned for a girl as young as Sadie. And what young girl had trouble deciding what to wear to her own wedding? Or serve at her own rehearsal dinner for that matter?

There was something off about the whole thing. Grace just couldn't put her finger on it.

She was saved from further comment when Gage barged in, not bothering to look up as he pawed through a drugstore bag. "Sadie, I brought you some Gatorade to help replace your electrolytes and some—"

He looked up, caught sight of Sadie, and immediately dropped the bag. Their eyes locked, and Grace suddenly felt like an intruder in the room.

Her thoughts vacillated between *oh boy, this isn't good*, and *oh, boy, this is awkward.*

Her mother caught her eye and her expression pleaded with Grace to do something. She sighed. Why was *she* always supposed to be the reasonable one?

"Hey, Gage," she said casually, "did you see Michael on your way up here? Wouldn't want the *groom* to see the *bride* in her dress before the big day."

She put an extra bit of snarkiness on the words *groom* and *bride* to drive her point home.

That seemed to do it. He blinked a couple of times and looked over at her. Shaking his head, he bent down and scooped up the bag, handing it to Grace. Turning on his heel, he stalked out, slamming the door behind him after muttering a hasty, "Sorry to intrude."

Grace glanced back at Sadie, who was still staring

unblinkingly at the spot Gage had vacated as if she could still see him there.

That's when she noticed the red splotches popping up all over Sadie's throat. "Um, Sadie, are you okay?"

Sadie's eyes widened as they flew to Grace's. She seemed to try—and fail—to pull a deep breath into her lungs. Shaking her head furiously, Sadie's hands flew to her throat, clawing at the lace there.

Grace and her mother and Ruthie must've looked like a *Three Stooges* sketch as they bumbled about the room, trying to help.

Ruthie stuck her head out the door and yelled for Gage, while Grace helped Sadie out of the restrictive dress's bodice and Sarah fanned her face.

Gage stormed back in and shoved them all out of the way as he took charge. He stopped in front of Sadie and stooped down a bit so he could look her in the eye. "Close your mouth and take a breath through your nose," he told her in his super-calm doctor voice.

She shook her head furiously, eyes locked on his, mouth opening and snapping shut like a landed trout.

"You can do it," he urged, quietly. "Close your mouth."

He let her struggle for another half a second before muttering, "Fuck."

And with that, he grabbed her face between his hands and

stepped closer to her. Their lips were only a heartbeat apart when he whispered, "Pretend it's just you and me here, Sadie. No one else. No reason to panic. Take a big, deep breath for me through your nose. Do it for *me*, okay?"

There wasn't anything overtly inappropriate about the words themselves, but the way they were looking at each other…there was something disturbingly intimate about it. Something that gave Grace a really bad feeling about the impending wedding. A *really* bad feeling.

But fortunately, it worked. Sadie sucked in a big breath through her nose.

"There you go," he murmured. "Again."

They looked like they were about three seconds away from kissing. Okay, this was officially *too* awkward.

"I'm finding it hard to believe Johns Hopkins taught you that particular method of helping a patient who's hyperventilating, Gage," Grace said in her driest of dry tones.

"Maybe I learned it from watching *ER* reruns," he said, tone equally dry, eyes still on Sadie.

Sadie let out a weak chuckle and stepped out of Gage's reach. "T-thank you, Gage. I don't know what happened there."

His eyes narrowed on her. "It was a panic attack. Have you ever had one before?"

She shook her head, then crossed her arms over her chest, seeming to notice for the first time that the bodice of her dress was around her waist and her white lacy bra was on full display.

Before *Gage* could notice Sadie's cleavage, Grace grabbed him, turned him around, and gave him a shove out the door. "Time to go, Dr. Love," she muttered. "Super-awkward half-naked bride time is over."

When they were outside the room with the door shut firmly behind them, Grace punched Gage in the arm, putting all her weight behind it.

"What the fuck?" Gage yelped, rubbing his arm.

"I was just about to ask you the same thing!" Grace hissed. "Jesus, what's going on between you two? You've been weird ever since you met her."

He scowled at her and ran a hand through his hair. "It's nothing. I'm dealing with it, OK?"

"Nothing? Are you kidding me? There was enough sexual tension in that room that I got a contact high." She shook her head and jerked her thumb toward Sadie's room. "*That* wasn't nothing. Are you trying to steal the bride, Gage?"

He looked disgusted. "Of course not. I'd never do that to Michael. It's just that…shit."

That's when she noticed his expression had shifted from disgusted and grumpy to defeated. She'd never seen Gage defeated before. "You like her," she said, gentling her tone. "You *really* like her."

He shoved a hand through his hair. "This is bullshit, right? It's just a physical thing. It has to be. There's no way you can start to have any real feelings for someone after a few days. Right?"

The desperation in his voice made her wish she could tell him he was right. That whatever he was feeling for Sadie—and whatever Sadie was feeling for him in return—would pass. But since she was experiencing the exact same thing with Nick…

His chin hit his chest when she didn't respond. "What the fuck do I do, Grace?"

She reared back as if he'd slapped her. Jesus, this was worse than she thought. Gage had never asked for advice from, well, *anyone* as far as she knew.

"Well," she said on a gusty sigh, knowing he wasn't going to like her advice, "I think you should stay away from her and let this thing play out."

His head shot up. "What if she marries him? It's a mistake."

"I know it is." She paused, rubbing her temples. "But she's obviously jittery and just getting over being sick. She's not in any kind of emotional shape to be leaving her fiancé for his *cousin*, for God's sake. We have a few days left before the wedding. Let me talk to Michael and Nick and see if we can *subtly* sort this…" *giant potential clusterfuck* "…*thing* out. Until then, you just stay away from her, okay?"

She supposed she'd have to take his frustrated grunt as agreement, because he'd already turned on his heel and stalked away. Ungrateful, antisocial, grumpy bastard, she thought.

"You're welcome!" she yelled down the hall at his retreating form.

Chapter Nineteen

"Hey, Nick," Grace shouted toward the open door between their rooms as she tossed her card key on the bed. "Can we talk for a…*oomph*."

Grace promptly forgot whatever she was going to say when Nick wrapped an arm around her waist, spun her around, and pinned her to the wall with his weight.

His mouth was on hers—urgent, hungry, demanding—before she could say anything else. Her fingers immediately tangled in his hair. His arms banded around her so tight they nearly forced the air from her lungs, and man, he felt so good against her—so hot, so strong, so safe. And his mouth…

Sweet Christ, did he know how to kiss. He kissed her like she was water and he was a man dying of thirst. The fact that he was with *her—k*issing *her*—was overwhelming and comforting and terrifying all at the same time. It was almost too much. *He* was almost too much.

He slid his fingertips up under her sweater, letting his big hands span her ribcage, thumbs dangerously close to her nipples which were, of course, on high alert.

He pulled back and rested his forehead against hers as she gasped for air, much like Sadie had during her panic attack. "I missed you," he whispered.

"I guess so," she choked out. "Jesus."

"And did you miss me?"

"Are you fishing?"

He grinned. "Like Brad Pitt in *A River Runs Through It.*"

She bit her lower lip. It was kind of embarrassing to admit how much she'd missed him. So instead, she opted for a prim, "I guess I'm not entirely *displeased* to see you."

His grin widened, and she let out a sharp burst of laughter as he dug his fingertips into her ribs and proceeded to tickle the hell out of her.

When she begged him to stop for fear that she'd pee herself, thankfully, he complied. "Was there something you wanted to talk about?" he asked.

She blinked up at him. Huh?

He smirked in a confident, cocky way that only really hot men could pull off. It was the kind of smirk that said, "I've seen you naked and I can see it all again any time I want."

Stupid, tall, smug, obscenely good-looking man.

"You came in here saying 'Hey, Nick, can we talk,'" he prompted.

Oh, right… "Has your sister ever had panic attacks before?"

His brow furrowed. "Not that I know of, why?"

Grace gave him a brief rundown of the panic attack, leaving out Gage's part in the whole thing. No need to start some kind of brooding, alpha-man war between the two of them. The whole thing was already weird enough as it was. Why add extra crazy to the mix?

When she was done, Nick took a step back and shoved a hand through his hair. "She's probably just nervous," he finally said. "I'm sure it's nothing to worry about."

Grace frowned. The bride breaking out in hives and having to be torn out of her wedding dress was nothing to worry about? This thing had *Runaway Bride* written all over it, as far as Grace was concerned. "I don't know, Nick. It was weird. And all the decisions she's been having so much trouble with? Have you really talked to her lately? I mean *really* talked? Are you sure she wants to do this?"

His hands shifted to his hips and she could tell he was a little irked by her questions. "Look, Grace, I know you don't approve of this marriage, and, hell, I can't say that I'm thrilled about it, either. But I know my sister. When other little girls dreamed of being ballerinas and princesses, she dreamed of being a wife and mother, of having a nice, normal family like yours. I'm going to believe she wants this marriage until I hear *her* say otherwise."

The emphasis he put on the word *her* made his point abundantly clear. He wasn't going to listen to conjecture. And she shouldn't either, really. She was a lawyer, for God's sake.

He put his hands on her shoulders and tipped his head down

so that she could look at him at eye-level. "Grace, Sadie deserves to be happy. You have no idea what she went through when we were growing up. She just…shit, she just deserves this, okay? Please don't actively interfere and look for ways to ruin it for her. And for your brother. Can you do that? Can you just…go with the flow for the next few days and let what happens *happen*? Please?"

It was the *please* that was ultimately her undoing. And the intense look he fixed her with. And the press of his hard body against hers.

Oh, who the hell am I kidding? I never stood a chance against this guy.

Grace nodded slowly. "Sure. I can, um, *go with the flow*. I won't interfere. You have my word."

His answering kiss was hard, fast, and left her leaning against the door to support herself, gasping for breath.

"You won't regret it," he whispered against her lips.

An image of Sadie and Gage eye-fucking each other popped into Grace's mind.

"God, I hope not," she muttered.

Chapter Twenty

Grace was willing to bet her favorite Kate Spade purse—and she really, *really* loved that bag—that it wasn't Sadie's idea to drag all of them to the Royal Landing amusement park, which was a good hour's drive from their resort.

Sadie's skin turned a sickly shade of pale as she gaped up in mute horror at a giant coaster called The Disemboweler. The poor girl obviously didn't share Michael's lifelong love of crazy, lose-your-lunch amusement park rides.

Grace couldn't say that she was exactly feeling it, either. After days of eating toast, bananas, and other mild fare, Grace's stomach (and metabolism) was ready to actively revolt if she didn't get some real food, real fast. And in Grace's world, real food meant grease, cholesterol, and anything fried to a nice, crispy, buttery brown.

Nick, bless his heart, gave her hand a squeeze. "What do you say we skip this one and get something to eat instead?"

She might have moaned and drooled a little before blurting, "Oh my God, yes. Please."

Michael frowned at her. "Jesus, Grace, he's offering you food, not orgasms. Chill out."

She shrugged, refusing to be embarrassed by her fervent enjoyment of junk food. But still, no way would she tell him she'd once had a nice little mini-orgasm while eating a deep-fried Twinkie at the State Fair. That fact was between her, Hostess, and a carney named Stan to whom she still sent a Christmas card every year. Good times.

Nick leaned down and Grace shivered as his lips brushed her ear. "Just so we're clear, orgasms aren't off the table. All you have to do is say the word."

That time, there was no "might have" about it. She definitely moaned. And drooled.

Nick chuckled while Michael grunted in disgust. "Ready to try this thing out, Sadie?"

Sadie let out a high-pitched nervous laugh that reminded Grace of an injured hyena she'd seen at the zoo once. "Sure. It looks…" Sadie gulped, "…great. The Disemboweler…that's quite a name. Let's do it."

Michael rubbed his hands together in childish glee, completely oblivious to his fiancée's apprehension. Grace frowned. "You don't have to go, Sadie," she said. "He can go by himself. You can come with us to get something to eat."

"Don't be stupid, Grace," Michael scoffed. "Sadie loves roller coasters. She wouldn't miss it, right, baby?"

"O-of course not." She offered Michael a tremulous smile as he slung an arm around her shoulders. "I wouldn't miss it."

Grace glanced up at Nick, whose furrowed brow confirmed what she already knew to be true. Sadie didn't like roller coasters.

So why was she pretending she did?

As Michael looped his arm around Sadie's waist and tugged her to the line of roughly a hundred thrill-seeking idiots who wanted a turn on The Disemboweler, Grace forced herself to shrug off her concerns.

It's Sadie's and Michael's business, not mine, she told herself. Go with the flow.

And as Nick reached down and laced his fingers through hers? Yeah, going with the flow pretty much *rocked,* she decided.

A few minutes later when Grace was tucking into a grilled cheese sandwich the size of her head and a ridiculously huge order of fries, a frazzled Gage showed up, staring after Sadie and Michael with a disgusted scowl on his face.

"What the fuck is that punk doing? Sadie's afraid of heights."

Nick frowned at him. "She told you that?"

Gage shoved a hand through his hair. "Yeah. Since the thing at your aunt's house when she was twelve, she can't even go in elevators. She always takes the stairs."

"What thing?" Grace asked.

"My aunt had a treehouse in her backyard," Nick murmured. "It was falling apart. I told her not to go up there, but Sadie was a headstrong kid. The floorboards snapped, and she fell and broke her arm. She's hated heights ever since."

She knew it went against the whole *go with the flow* thing, but the lawyer in Grace couldn't help but ask, "So why didn't she tell Michael that? I mean, he thinks she loves roller coasters, and she didn't correct him."

Nick's frown deepened. "She's never been one to talk about her feelings. Maybe she's trying to overcome her fear or something."

Grace followed Gage's gaze to Sadie in line for the ride. The poor kid looked like she was going to puke. Michael looked totally oblivious.

Yeah, this is a guy who's ready for marriage.

"Are you guys helping her out of this, or am I?" Gage growled.

Grace shifted her eyes to Nick. A muscle in his jaw tensed, but he said nothing. *Great, no help there.* "It's not your business, Gage," she said quietly. "But…if you can find a way to help *subtly*, I say go for it."

He turned on his heel and marched his stiff shoulders and squinty, annoyed eyes right up to Michael. After a few seconds of heated conversation, Sadie gave Michael a quick kiss on the cheek and walked over to Nick, Gage hot on her heels. Michael stubbornly crossed his arms over his chest and held his place in line.

Grace smiled at Sadie as she sat down at their table and snagged a fry off Nick's tray. "Problem?"

Sadie smiled back. "Nope. Gage just didn't think that roller coasters were a good idea, since we're still recovering from food poisoning."

She glanced over at Gage and struggled not to roll her eyes at the lame-ass excuse he'd come up with. He gave her a sharp stare, telling her with his eyes not to contradict him.

"I'm sure that's true," she eventually said, striving for her most benign tone. It was the same tone she used with clients who were just *sure* none of their employees would ever steal from them, that they'd know if something like that was going on.

For the record, more often than not, they *were*, and they *didn't.*

As Sadie sat down and started talking to Nick, Grace caught Gage's eye again and mouthed, "Lame."

He scratched the side of his nose. With his middle finger.

Real mature, Gage. Real mature.

Not to be…*out-matured*, Grace brushed her hair off her forehead with her middle finger, then one-upped him by crossing her eyes at him.

Take that.

Then she realized she was having a one-finger salute fight with her almost thirty-year-old cousin and suddenly didn't feel so proud of herself anymore. For some reason, Gage always brought out her inner twelve-year-old.

Later that evening, after Michael had ridden every ride in the park and Grace had eaten her body weight in fried yummy goodness, they all went back to the hotel. In the elevator on the way to their rooms, Nick said, "I might be willing to admit that you were on to something with my sister. I'll talk to her."

Grace let out an inward sigh of relief. Outwardly, she merely nodded and said, "Whatever you think is best. No pressure."

She was rewarded for her easy-going response with a kiss that damn near stopped her heart.

Hmmm. Maybe there was something to this whole "go with the flow" thing after all. Who knew?

Chapter Twenty-one

Dinner that night wasn't a complete train wreck, Nick thought to himself rather happily.

Sure, Gage and Sadie still had a disturbing amount of nearly R-rated eye contact, and Sarah still looked at Nick like she was mentally castrating him. But Brad hadn't shown up until dessert, ("Gee, was I supposed to invite him?" Gage had said, completely devoid of sincerity. Nick had discreetly knuckle-bumped him on that one) and Ruthie had only insulted gays, the Irish, and the Catholic clergy (long story) a few times. She'd made one waiter cry, but the 35% tip Nick had given him seemed to make him feel better. (There was nothing he could do to make it up to the gays, Irish, and the clergy. They were on their own.)

"Did you talk to Sadie?" Grace asked as they got out of the elevator to head back to their rooms.

He nodded. "She's just nervous about meeting all of you and wants to make a good impression. I don't think there's anything to worry about."

She frowned up at him. "You led the witness, didn't you?"

"What does that mean?"

"You asked her questions, she didn't have good answers, so you made up your own answers, and she readily agreed with you. You led her to the answer you wanted. That's called leading the witness."

She was more right than he cared to admit. His talk with Sadie had been a little tense. When he'd started asking about her relationship with Michael and why she was suddenly so damned agreeable about everything, she'd gotten defensive. And when he'd asked about what was going on with her and Gage—and with the sexual tension that practically choked the air out of the room when they were together—she'd shut down on him completely.

But he didn't really want to admit any of that to Grace at the moment. So, instead he said, "God, you're hot when you *lawyer* like that."

Because that was true, too. Grace was damn hot when she lawyered. And looked at him. And said his name. And breathed in his general direction.

Her answering laugh reached right down into his pants and grabbed hold of his dick, giving it a nice, firm tug. "Yeah, that's exactly what they teach you in law school. How to argue and be hot at the same time."

He was about to say something else—something terribly witty and charming, he was sure—when Grace stumbled to a stop beside him. He followed her gaze and couldn't hold back a disgusted sigh.

DoucheBrad.

The little fucker was leaning against Grace's door, waiting for her.

Brad straightened to his full height—which still only put the top of his head to just about Nick's shoulder, so, *ha*!—as they approached. He didn't spare so much as a glance in Nick's direction, instead giving Grace his full, bespectacled attention.

"Grace, may I please have a moment of your time?" he intoned in that uppity British accent of his that grated on Nick's nerves like sandpaper.

Nick shook his head in disgust. N*ow* the guy was all polite and respectful. *Where were all those good manners when you were fucking around on Grace, doucheBrad?*

Beside him, Grace sighed. "Brad, I really don't know what else we have to say to each other. The divorce was finalized months ago. Final means *final*, as far as I'm concerned."

Nick did a mental fist pump. *Take that, doucheBrad.*

The little fucker cleared his throat and pushed his glasses up with his index finger before fixing her with a look Nick had only ever seen puppies at the pound accomplish before. "Please, Grace," Brad said. "Only a moment. That's all I ask."

Pathetic, Nick thought, unable to stop his upper lip from curling up in derision. If he thought Grace was going to fall for sad puppy-dog eyes and a half-assed, sorrowful…

Grace let out another deep sigh and laid her hand on Nick's arm. "Nick, can you excuse us for a just a moment?"

Wait…what? He shook his head in disbelief. Clearly, he hadn't heard her right. "Grace, you can't be serious. How can you even *consider* giving this guy—"

Her eyes narrowed on him ever so slightly. "Nick, I'm completely serious. The only thing I'm *considering* is having an adult conversation with a man I used to be married to. Why are you looking at me like I've just sprouted a third breast?"

The third breast thing threw him off his train of thought for a minute, but he rallied as quickly as possible. "This is a guy that jerked you around. Treated you like crap. A guy that showed up here, unannounced, at a family event to try and win you back. And just like *that*"—he snapped his fingers—"you're going to give him what he wants? I thought you were tougher than that."

"Now, see here," Brad sputtered.

"Shut up, Brad," Nick and Grace hissed in unison.

Grace's spine stiffened as she glared up at Nick. "Having a conversation with the man doesn't mean I forgive him for everything he did. What do you think is going to happen if I talk to him? That I'm going to fall on my back with my legs up in the air just because he utters a half-assed apology or two?"

Nick leaned into her space with a sneer and said, "Why not? I didn't even have to apologize to get you to wrap your legs around me in that elevator."

If he could've reversed the earth's rotation to turn back time like Superman did in that old Christopher Reeve movie to snatch the words back, Nick would have done it. It was a horrible thing to say. And shit, he didn't even mean it. He was just jealous and pissed off. But the words were out there now, and by the way Grace's face completely shut down, it was way too late to call them back.

True to form, Grace composed herself quickly, her features taking on an icy calm that made Nick way more nervous than any glare or well-deserved punch to the junk ever could. "Well, I guess there's really no point in discussing this further if that's what you think of me. Goodbye, Nick."

That very final sounding goodbye knifed him right in the heart. Moving quickly so she didn't have time to punch him (like he so richly deserved), he slid his hand around the back of her neck and pulled her into a short, hard kiss on the mouth. "It's good*night*, Grace. Not goodbye. We're not done yet. Not by a longshot."

Chapter Twenty-two

Grace stared at the empty spot in the hallway where Nick had just been, still struggling to comprehend what the hell happened.

Everything had been going so well. Dinner had been lovely. Well, not *lovely*, she supposed. No one had gotten hurt, which put it at least in the top five family dinners she'd ever had. But *Nick* had been lovely. Kind, attentive, funny, sexy as all hell…Nick O'Connor had been a picture-perfect dinner date.

Until he'd turned into a six-foot-something, 190-pound, Incredible Hulk of jealous dumbfuckery.

Ugh. To insinuate that she was some kind of easily manipulated skank who'd wrap her legs around anyone who whispered a few kind words to her was beyond insulting. He was lucky she hadn't throat-punched him. Jerk.

But he didn't really lie, the lawyer half of her brain argued. *You* did *wrap your legs around him after some kind words, only a few days after meeting him.*

"Oh, shut up. No one asked you," she muttered.

Brad cleared his throat and fidgeted nervously with the cuffs of his white dress shirt. "But I didn't say anything, darling."

Jeez, she'd forgotten for a moment that Brad was still there. Again: ugh.

Grace pinched the bridge of her nose and held in yet another put-upon sigh. She was already regretting her decision to give Brad a few moments of her time. And not because of the fight with Nick, but because she truly didn't care what he had to say. Any apology he could offer was years overdue at this point, and she couldn't imagine any circumstances under which she'd consider letting him back into her life.

Like, even if the zombie apocalypse hit and her very life depended on remarrying Brad, Grace was pretty certain she'd follow in the footsteps of Sasha on *The Walking Dead* and end it all. That's how much she *didn't* want another chance with Brad.

But, she was here, and now that she'd taken a stand against Nick regarding her right to have this conversation, Grace imagined she might as well tough it out and listen to what Brad had to say. Maybe he'd do everyone a favor and go home after he'd said his peace.

With great reluctance, Grace said, "You wanted a moment of my time and you got it, Brad. Say what you have to say, because I'm tired and ready to go to bed."

Brad laid a cool hand on her shoulder. "Are you alright? That was an ugly scene."

Grace felt her back teeth grind together and was powerless to stop it. Insincere bastard, she thought. He looked like he might pull a muscle or something trying to hold back his inner glee at having managed to run Nick off. "I'm fine, Brad. Why are you here?"

He took a step forward. "I think it's time that we talked, don't you?"

She took a step back, shaking his hand off her shoulder in the process. "Sure. But I've been wrong before. I mean, I would've thought you'd want to talk to me *before* you decided to start cheating on me, but…" she trailed off, shrugging.

He did a little man-pout that was somehow pathetic and irritating all at the same time. "You're going to make this difficult for me, aren't you?"

"What possible reason would I have at this point to make your life any easier?" she asked, perplexed.

"I made a mistake with Destiny. I think you owe it to me—to us—to give our marriage another try," Brad said, somehow managing to make the ridiculous words sound perfectly reasonable.

But then it hit her…

"Her name was *Destiny*? You cheated on me with a woman named *Destiny*?"

He blinked owlishly at her, obviously unsure how to respond in a way that wouldn't incite her to violence. But it suddenly occurred to Grace that she really wasn't all that pissed-off any more. Sure, it stung a little that he'd thrown her away—thrown their marriage away—for a woman who probably wore acrylic heels and wrapped her legs around a pole while shaking her ass to Def Leppard's *Pour Some Sugar on Me* on the weekends. But after the drama of getting to the wedding and getting sick, then the fight she'd just had with Nick, it all seemed pretty silly at the moment. Insignificant.

Maybe it was the stress of the day, or maybe she'd had too much wine with dinner, but whatever the reason, Grace laughed out loud. She laughed until she snorted. She laughed until she slumped over and had trouble catching her breath.

Brad took a step back, looking at her like a baby bunny eyeing a hungry wolf. "Grace, I hardly think this is a laughing matter," he muttered. "I'm lonely without you, darling. Destiny doesn't…she doesn't understand me. She doesn't *get* me like you did."

Well, that put a pin in the funny, she thought sourly. He was still the same selfish bastard he always was. He missed what she gave him, he didn't miss *her*. "Well, what did you think would happen when you started banging a woman half your age, Brad? She's only nineteen! Of course she doesn't *get* you," she said, shaking her head. "All your pop culture references are old-man references to her. You might as well call her a pesky kid and yell at her to get off your lawn, Grandpa."

A sick puppy at the pound couldn't have given her a more sorrowful look than the one Brad leveled on her. "I made a mistake. What I had with Destiny was purely physical. It could never be anything more than that with someone like her. I understand that now." The sad puppy look morphed into something infinitely more bitter as he added, "Surely *you* understand that now as well."

And just like that, contrite Brad was replaced with doucheBrad. The world suddenly made sense again. "What makes you think that my attraction to Nick is purely physical?"

He snorted. "Please. Give me some credit. He's not your type."

"Why? Because he's funny and kind and sexy? Yes, clearly that's not my *usual* type," she said, gesturing to Brad. "But I'm thinking maybe it's time to change things up a bit."

Brad's face flushed red and he began rolling up the sleeves of his dress shirt. "So is that why you aren't willing to give us another try? *Him*? We hit a rough patch in our relationship and you take up with the first piece of trailer trash you stumble upon?"

Only the fear that Brad would press charges kept Grace from punching him in the face. But her fingers ached with the need to do just that. She settled for poking him in the chest with her index finger hard enough that delicate-skinned Brad would bruise like a week-old peach.

"First of all," she began, "we didn't hit a 'rough patch.' You screwed around on me and we got divorced. Second of all, I didn't *take up* with trailer trash. I *took up* with a man who stayed up for days in a row, talking to me and holding my hair back for me while I puked. *I took up* with a man who makes me feel *alive* for the first time in years." She leaned in and poked him again before adding, "I *took up* with a man who practically made me come just by kissing me." His flinch was so intensely gratifying that she smiled at him (although it was probably more like an unfriendly baring of teeth, if she was being honest with herself). "So, *no*, you don't get to compare what I have with Nick to what you had—or still have, probably—with *Destiny*."

Brad reared back as if she'd slapped him and made a show of pressing imaginary wrinkles out of his shirt while he composed himself. "Well, I can see you're clearly not in the right frame of mind to discuss this now. We'll talk again tomorrow."

"There's nothing left to talk about."

But Brad probably hadn't heard her, because he'd turned and stormed off as if the hounds of hell were nipping at his heels.

With a weary sigh, Grace let herself into her room, noticing immediately that the door between her room and Nick's was closed. *Jerk*, she thought. Just because she'd defended him to Brad didn't mean she wasn't still mad at Nick for what he'd said tonight.

Not that it mattered, since he was obviously just as mad at her as she was at him.

Men sucked, she decided instantly. Maybe she should have taken Nick's suggestion to give girls a try a little more seriously.

Chapter Twenty-three

Twenty minutes later, Grace was standing in front of the minibar in her room, contemplating scarfing down a king-sized Snickers bar and chasing it down with a little bottle of vodka, when Nick knocked on the door separating their rooms. Her heart leapt up in excitement (*Let him in! Let him in!*) while her brain immediately went into self-defense mode (*He's an ass! Ignore him!*).

With one last look at the minibar—maybe she'd chase that Snickers bar down with *two* little bottles of vodka. Hadn't she earned the right after the day she'd just had?—she walked over and leaned against the door, crossing her arms over her chest.

"What do you want, Nick?" she asked, putting as much "suck it, asshole" into her tone as possible.

"Can we talk, Grace? Please?"

The "please" was a nice touch, but it wasn't enough to take the chill off what he'd said to her earlier. "Sure. Talk."

"Will you open the door so I can see you?"

"No."

She heard him sigh. "I deserve that. I'm so sorry for what I said earlier, Grace. I didn't even mean it. I was just so…jealous and fucked-up about the thought of you being with that asshat. I wanted to tear him apart for even *thinking* he deserved to breathe the same air as you, and all I ended up doing was treating you like shit. Do you think you could ever forgive me?"

She wanted to tell him he was forgiven, because what he'd just said was probably the best apology she'd ever heard. Hell, Brad had *cheated* on her and hadn't delivered half the apology Nick just had—and all he'd wrong done was talk out his ass for a minute! Who *hadn't* been guilty of that at some point?

But while her heart wanted to immediately forgive him, her brain cautioned against it. That very apology—and her gut reaction to it—was proof that Nick was dangerous. Brad's betrayal had hurt. But if this *thing* she had with Nick went further, when he left her (because let's face it, everyone left eventually), she'd be destroyed.

How could she knowingly hand that kind of power over to anyone?

Grace let out a sigh of her own. "I'd like to forgive you, Nick. But…maybe this all happened for a reason. What you said was true. I did get involved with you really quickly. Too quickly. Maybe it's time we step back and re-evaluate this thing."

He was quiet for so long Grace started to wonder if he'd walked away or if he even planned to respond at all. Then he said, "Are you telling me that you want some space? Are you giving me an it's-not-you-it's-me speech?"

Grace blinked. Wow, he was right. That's exactly what she

was doing. She'd been on the receiving end a time or two, but hadn't ever delivered one herself. And if she had to guess? She'd be willing to bet Nick never had a speech like that aimed at him, either.

Well, there was a first time for everything, she supposed.

With a nod that was entirely useless because he couldn't see it, she said, "Yes. I suppose I am."

She was pretty sure her heart face-palmed, all while her brain patted her on the back and offered platitudes about how there were plenty of other fish in the sea.

Grace flinched as there was a *thunk* on the door. It was a fairly distinct *thunk*, too. The *thunk* of a forehead dropping to the wood in defeat.

"Grace," he said in that low, gravelly tone that never failed to reduce her knees to mush. "Don't do this. Please let me in."

There was more to that request than the obvious. He wasn't just asking her to open her door. He was asking her to open her heart to him. To take a chance. To let her heart do the thinking for once.

And, *God*, how she wanted to. It'd be so *easy* to let Nick in. To lose herself in him. It'd be good, too. For a while, at least. But then…

"I'm sorry, Nick," she choked out past the lump of emotion that had settled in her throat. "I can't. I'm done talking about this.

Please just go."

Grace didn't even wait for a reply. Instead, she shut off her light and threw herself down on the bed, wrapping her arms around her middle in an attempt to ward off the chill that had settled into her bones.

She'd done the right thing. Nick was too…*everything* for her. They didn't belong together. It didn't matter that he turned her on and made her laugh and had a huge heart. Letting him go now, before she got too attached, was the right thing to do.

But you already are attached, dumbass.

Jesus, had that come from her heart or her brain?

Okay, stay calm, she told herself, sucking in a deep breath. Think this through logically. Look at the pros and cons.

Pro number one for letting Nick go before things got any more complicated between them: Nick lived in Chicago and she lived in LA. Even if everything worked out between them (and that was a giant, massive, life-sized *if*) the best they could hope for was a long-distance relationship, because she couldn't leave her practice in LA to follow him to Chicago (she was on track to be the youngest partner in the firm's history, for God's sake), and she wouldn't ask him to uproot his life to follow her to LA.

Con for letting Nick go now: No more long talks about nothing and everything. The kind of talks that made her laugh until she nearly cried. The kind of talks that made her feel more alive and connected to another human being than she'd ever felt with anyone else. Those talks were so…intimate, and going back to a life without that kind of intimacy—the kind she was pretty sure she'd never had with another anyone else—was truly terrifying.

Pro for letting Nick go now before they got too involved: The chances of her ending up an emotionally crippled shell of her former self, drowning in mint mocha chip ice cream and vodka to dull the pain of losing him at some point in her not-so-distant future were all but nil. Suffer a little bit now, save herself infinitely greater pain later. It seemed like a reasonable trade-off.

But then, of course, there was the other con for letting Nick go now: Not ever getting to have sex with him. Never getting to know what it felt like to be with him, skin-to-skin, surrounded by him, losing herself to him as he drove her to the edge of sanity and beyond…

I'm not looking for a relationship.

Yeah, but what would you do if you found one?

Images of the past few days with Nick raced through her mind like montage clips from a cheesy romantic comedy. Nick smirking at her across the table in that airport holding room, Nick paying for a stranger's dinner and blushing when she saw evidence of what a nice guy he was, Nick protecting her from Cletus the creepy motel night manager, Nick holding her and taking care of her when she was too sick to move, Nick kissing the holy hell out of her in that elevator…

“Damn,” Grace muttered. “I’ve found a relationship.”

And that was pretty much when her heart told her brain, with all its logic and pro/con lists, to go screw itself. How could she possibly let him go *now*? She’d been a fool to even consider it.

A cocktail of dread and panic coursed through her veins as she considered the possibility that he might not want her anymore. She had stiff-armed him away from her pretty hard. What if he was in the hotel bar right now, picking up some hot, willing woman who wasn’t all fifty shades of fucked-up like Grace was?

Driven by panic, Grace shot up off the bed and raced to the door separating their rooms. Without giving any thought to what she might see if he wasn’t alone in that room, Grace yanked the door open and…

Let out a shocked gasp when she found Nick standing right there, head down, arms braced on the doorframe above his head.

He hadn’t moved when she told him to go away.

Nick lifted his head slowly, and when his eyes met hers, Grace knew there was no turning back. The hurt, the longing, the confusion, the need…everything she was feeling was looking right back at her from the depths of his fathomless blue eyes.

She opened her mouth, but whatever she was going to say was lost forever when he grabbed her, yanked her into his arms and kissed the ever-lovin' hell out of her.

Chapter Twenty-four

Grace didn't even hesitate. She threw herself into the kiss as wholeheartedly as he did. Maybe a little too wholeheartedly, she admitted to herself as he staggered back a step under the onslaught of her full body weight against him. But true to form, he righted himself quickly, his hands slipping down to her ass, pulling her tightly against him.

Nick flipped her around, pressing her back against the wall in his room. He kissed her hard and with a desperation she could only attribute to fear of being pushed away again.

Not that there was any chance of *that* happening at the moment.

He pulled back just far enough to rest his forehead against hers, his breathing ragged. "I'm so sorry, Grace. I didn't mean what I said."

Less talking, more kissing, she wanted to say, but his mouth seemed to have some kind of gravitational pull, because she couldn't help but go after his lips again. He held her back, though. "I mean it," he said in a voice so rough it sounded like it'd been beaten against rocks since they last spoke. "Do you forgive me?"

"Only if you don't stop kissing me."

He raised his head and looked down into her eyes, and Grace knew she was *this* close to convincing him to surrender. And damned if seeing that near-surrender in *this* man's eyes didn't make her feel like the sexiest siren ever to have lived. It was a heady, dangerous feeling. She could get used to it, grow dependent on it, so, so fast.

But that was a worry for another day. There just wasn't room for worry between them at the moment. Only heat, forgiveness, passion, and need.

He closed his eyes and let out a hoarse groan. "You're killing me. Don't we need to talk about this?"

She was pretty sure she was going to die if she didn't get him inside her soon, so she just shook her head. "Not now."

He slid his hand under her hair to firmly but gently grip her nape. "We *will* talk about this later," he said, his tone brooking no argument.

Yes! Grace did a mental fist pump. She had him!

"Later," she agreed. "Much later."

Her entire body hummed with electricity as he moaned into her mouth and kissed her again. It wasn't long before their kisses grew feverish and frantic, their breathing labored.

Grace had never been the type to lose control, but with Nick, control was nothing more than a distant memory—and not an entirely *pleasant* distant memory. If this was what it felt like to let go with Nick, Grace realized there was no going back. She might just be officially ruined for all other men, and she hadn't even gotten him inside her yet.

Nick was the first to break the kiss. But her moan of protest turned into a shocked squeal as he bent down, put his shoulder into her stomach and neatly upended her, tossing her over his shoulder, caveman-style. In a few long, purposeful strides, he reached his bed, where he dumped her unceremoniously onto the mattress.

Her body barely even had time to bounce once before he was on her, holding his weight off her as he kissed her again, nudging her thighs apart with his knee. Grace gasped into his mouth as he lowered his body onto hers, then she let out an embarrassing sound—something needy and desperate and guttural—when he rocked his hips gently into her.

"Jesus Christ," he groaned between kisses. "That is the sexiest damn sound I've ever heard in my life."

Oh, okay. Maybe she shouldn't be embarrassed by that sound after all.

Which was a good thing, because she started making that sound on a continuous loop as Nick slid his lips down over her neck. While his tongue traced the hollow at the base of her throat, his hands worked the knot at the waist of her robe free. When the thick layers of terrycloth were peeled back and she was completely bared to his gaze, she could actually feel the weight and heat of his stare gliding all over every inch of her skin.

All. Over.

But even as her skin warmed and tingled under the intensity of his stare, old insecurities reared their ugly heads. She'd never lost that freshman fifteen—okay, twenty—she'd picked up at Notre Dame. Brad had certainly never let her hear the end of *that*, especially when he bought her a gym membership for Christmas and an elliptical machine for her birthday. (The elliptical machine doubled nicely as a rack to dry her sweaters on, though, so at least it was practical. The gym membership had been a total waste.) And here she was, laid out like a sacrificial offering to a guy who was built like a Greek god…

He shook his head slowly and lifted awe-filled eyes to hers. "I've never seen anything so beautiful. You're perfect, Grace."

And he meant every word, she realized. To him, she truly was perfect. It didn't matter if her thighs jiggled, or her ass was dimply. He thought she was beautiful just the way she was. Tears filled her eyes, but she impatiently blinked them away.

Grace released the death grip she had on the sheets and leaned up, taking his face in her hands as she kissed him. "Where have you been all my life?"

He wrapped his arms around her and pulled her tightly against him. "Just waiting for you, angel. Just waiting for you."

Well, if that wasn't the best aphrodisiac in the world, she

didn't know what was. Grace reached down and tugged impatiently on the hem of his shirt. "Off. Now. Need."

He chuckled. "Yes, ma'am," he said as he reached behind him, snagged the back of his shirt and tugged it over his head in that way that only guys could ever seem to accomplish. If Grace tried that, she'd end up with her shirt stuck on her ears and her arms trapped like they were in a straightjacket.

The shirt hadn't even hit the floor before she got her hands on him, letting her fingertips trace the contours of his chest before shifting and letting them bump over the ridges of his abs, all—two, four, six—*eight* of them. And to think she'd sworn after watching *300* that eight-packs were only possible with CGI.

Other than the tightening of his muscles and his shallow breathing, he stayed perfectly still while she touched him. It was absolute, glorious torture. Beautiful and agonizing at the same time.

She wanted more of him and she wanted it *now*. With a growl of frustration, she hooked her hand behind his head and yanked him down on her, pressing her mouth to his once more, fervently, feverishly.

She felt his smile against her mouth and it made her want to snag his lower lip between her teeth and nip the hell out of it—just to let him know she meant business. But she didn't dare for fear he'd stop altogether.

But he must have sensed how close he was to losing his lower lip because he murmured. "Relax, angel. We have all night."

All night? she screamed inwardly. She couldn't go on like this all night! She needed more *now*. It had been too long. Far, far too long.

But that and all other rational thought left the building when his hand slid down her stomach before slipping deftly between her legs.

Grace might have blacked out a little at that point. All she knew for sure was that he touched her like he'd been gifted an owner's manual for her body. He knew just how to touch her to reduce her to a quivering, panting, whimpering puddle with no coherent thoughts other than how much she wanted—no, *needed*—to come.

"Please," she said on a desperate exhale, then nearly sobbed like a baby when his hand slowed as he listened to her. "You need to be in me *now*."

"Not yet," he murmured.

She would've protested, but her eyes rolled back in her head and words escaped her when he dipped his head and sucked one of her nipples into his mouth. After shifting to give her other breast his attention—*hallelujah and thank you, Jesus*—he lifted his head to watch her reaction as his hand started moving again.

Grace bit down on her lower lip and squeezed her eyes shut, determined not to make any more noises that would let him know just how close she was to coming. She just couldn't take the risk of him trying to slow things down again. But he must have been on to her, because just when her legs began to quiver, just when she was right *there*, his fingers slowed again.

With a roar of frustrated outrage, Grace slapped her hands down on the mattress. "Motherfucker!" she cried.

The motherfucker kissed her jawline. "You have no idea how sexy you are right now," he said, licking the spot right below her ear.

Grace sucked in a deep breath through her nose. "Then why are you torturing me?"

"You think it's not torture for me, too?" he said with a tight-sounding chuckle. "I'm trying my damnedest to go slow. I've been thinking about dead puppies and baseball stats since you opened that door to keep from shredding your clothes like a fucking animal and pounding you into the wall."

Grace shifted under him and practically purred at the thought of him pounding her into the wall. "And that would be bad?"

"It'd be *great*. Awesome. Reality-altering, most likely. But it wouldn't be fucking romantic, and I was kind of going for romantic here, Grace. I'm tryin' to make this last."

A little bit of Jersey was seeping back into his voice, letting her know he wasn't as calm, cool, and in control as he'd let her believe up until that point. Thank God.

Reaching up, she cupped her hand around the back of his neck and yanked his head down so that their mouths were only a whisper apart before she said, "Nick, I need you to do something for me."

"Anything," he said without hesitation.

Again, *thank God.*

Putting every bit of seriousness into her tone as humanly possible, she looked him dead in the eye and said, "It's been a really long time since I've had sex, Nick, and I need you to fuck me. Hard and fast. Getting pounded into the wall sounds *perfect* to me. We can worry about romance later. And there will *definitely* be a later, because I guarantee you, one time will *not* be enough."

His eyes went dark and his expression turned nothing short of feral—and Grace knew a moment of trepidation. Had she bitten off more than she could chew with this one? But his next words shut down that train of thought faster than she could draw her next breath.

"Then brace yourself, angel. This might get rough."

Yeeeessss.

Thank God, Nick thought as Grace bit her lip and nodded her agreement.

For all his good intentions of taking things slow, of showing Grace how much she meant to him and how much he respected her, he wasn't sure how much longer he could've held out on her. It was getting to the point that not even dead puppies and obscure baseball stats could keep his baser instincts at bay. The need to be inside her was starting to overrule every other need he had, including the need for air. If he had to choose at the moment, he'd definitely take Grace over air.

He stripped and got a condom on faster than he ever had in his life, all under her watchful, lust-filled eyes. Shit, just the weight of her gaze on him was enough to damn-near make him come. She was right about one thing for sure.

This would *not* be their only time together. He'd never get enough of Grace Montgomery. Not ever.

When he reached under her and lifted her off the bed, she squealed, but didn't back down. Her fingers threaded through his hair, fingernails scraping along his scalp. Chills swept over his skin. God, it felt so good to have her hands on him, her tongue stroking his.

Her legs looped around his waist and tightened as he put her back against the wall and leaned into her, pinning her there with his weight, rocking his hips against hers. With a groan, she dug her heels into his back and pulled him closer. "Yes," she whispered against his mouth. "Now."

No more than half a second later, he was starting to slide into her, his hands cupping her ass, her fingernails digging into his shoulders. Her mouth fell open on a hiss as he slowly started to lower her onto his cock.

His thoughts at that point devolved quickly. *Tight, wet, hot, heaven.* Jesus. Had anything, anyone, ever felt this good, this *right*, in his life?

She squirmed and let out a desperate whimper. "Oh, God. I want you so bad, but it's been too long and you're way bigger than I'm used to. I don't know if I can take all of you like this."

Well, shit, if that didn't do wonders for the old ego, nothing ever would. "You can." *You will.* "I'll stop whenever you want me to. You're in charge."

But her fears were unfounded. Her head thunked back against the wall and her eyes fell shut as she proved him right. She took every last inch.

"Are you okay?" he asked.

Her only answer came in the form of an unintelligible grunt. "Do you want me to stop?" he clarified.

Please say no. Please say no. Please say no.

Grace's eyes flew open and her nails dug into his shoulders. "God, no! Don't stop. Please don't stop."

That was pretty much all he needed to hear.

Nick drove into her, hard and fast, just like she'd asked. She cried out so loud with every thrust he was pretty sure their neighbors would be complaining any minute. Not that he cared. Nothing short of the National Guard was going to stop him at this point.

Their combined desire was damn near animalistic.

"I swear I'll fuck you all night if you want me to," he whispered in her ear, his voice so rough and urgent he barely recognized it as his own. "I'll make you come so many times, so hard, you'll see fucking stars. I won't stop until every fucking guest on this floor knows my name because you'll be screaming it so loud."

She let out a gasp/moan combo that reached down and gripped his balls in a velvet vice. Every muscle in his body tightened and burned, and he knew he couldn't last much longer like this. He had to focus if he wanted to make sure she was taken care of before he got off.

Nick shifted so that both his hands were under her again and pulled her in tighter against him, flexing his hips at the same time to make sure the base of his cock hit her clit with every thrust.

"Oh my God," she cried, her eyes drifting shut. "Don't stop! Please don't stop."

As if *that* was even an option at this point.

Her head dropped to his shoulder and her hands clutched desperately at his biceps as she finally—*finally*—came, screaming his name just like he'd promised she would, her body tightening and pulsing around him. And that's when he lost control.

If he'd ever really *had* any with her, that is.

He came harder than he ever had in his life, buried as deep within her as he could get, with her face pressed into his neck, her heart pounding against his, her harsh, rasping breaths a perfect mirror of his own. It was as close to a perfect moment as Nick imagined he'd ever had or *would* ever have.

Being with Grace, right from the start, had been fun. No matter how complicated their personal and family situations were, being with Grace was easy. But *this*, this feeling of *peace* that he felt right now wasn't something he had any experience with. Being with Grace was like coming home.

Maybe it was that uncharacteristically deep thought, or maybe it was the fact that he was most likely dehydrated, but whatever the reason, that's when Nick's legs gave out.

Stumbling, completely spent, he dropped to his knees, dragging Grace down with him. She squealed and clung to him like a sloth, knocking him flat on his back on the hotel carpet.

Shit, he thought, waiting for her to get pissed at him. Talk about a mood-killer.

Then, in typical Grace fashion, she did something that shocked the hell out of him.

She started laughing.

Chapter Twenty-six

The rest of the night went pretty much exactly as Nick had promised. Her naked ass had been on every surface of both their hotel rooms. A few of their neighbors complained to hotel management about the noise, and one of them (*cough*Gage*cough) resorted to banging on the wall and shouting creative, anatomically impossible threats at them in an effort to get them to turn down the volume.

Normally, Grace would be embarrassed by the fact that everyone on their floor knew exactly what they'd been doing all night. (And, yes, they did indeed all know Nick's name now) But at the moment? She couldn't care any less if she tried. It seemed that, oh, twenty or so orgasms could wring shame and embarrassment right out of a girl.

And sometime around six in the morning, as she dropped limply onto Nick's sweaty chest, completely spent, possibly dehydrated, and most likely ruined for all other men, shame was the farthest thing from her mind.

"Holy God," Grace panted, pressing her forehead into the spot where Nick's neck met his shoulder, taking a moment to appreciate the masculine scent of his skin, which was also all over every inch of her own body. Every. Inch. "What the hell was all *that*?"

Nick chuckled and wrapped his arms around her. "That's

what happens when you have days and days of foreplay."

This was the first time they'd talked all night. Well, actual conversations, at least. Grace didn't imagine the *oh-God-yes-right-there* and *Jesus-yes-harder-faster exchanges* they'd had really counted as *conversations.* And their time between condom changes had mostly been spent on kissing, gently roving hands, and some really intense eye contact. No one gave sexy eye contact like Nick O'Connor.

Grace shivered. Yep. It was official. She was ruined for all other men.

Nick must've mistaken her shiver for a chill, because he reached down, pulled the balled-up comforter off the floor, and draped it over her bare back. The fact that he was considerate, thoughtful, *and* a sex god was going to be a *major* problem for her when they both went their separate ways after the wedding.

The thought alone brought tears to Grace's eyes and she was forced to choke back a sob.

"Hey," Nick said, shoving his hands into her hair and gently pulling back so that she was forced to lift her head and meet his gaze. "What's wrong? Don't tell me you're having regrets already."

"Regrets?" Who the fuck would ever regret the kind of night they'd just had? "Are you *insane*? No way. It's just that…"

He kissed her forehead, which was like an ice pick to her heart. Why the hell did he have to be so damn *perfect*?

"It's just that what, angel?" he prompted gently.

"I'm just going to really miss you, is all," she blurted, horrified that the tears she'd been blinking back now rolled down her cheeks and over her chin before landing in pathetic little puddles on his chest. "When the wedding is over and I go back to LA and you go back to Chicago, I'm really going to miss you, okay?"

His eyes roamed over her face as if her features held the secrets to all of life's mysteries. When he brushed her tears away with his thumbs, her heart cracked open just a little more. "You don't have to," he whispered.

She frowned, confused. "I don't have to what?"

"Miss me." He shrugged. The gesture was careless, but the look in his eyes let her know his words were anything but. "I can work from LA just as easily as I can from Chicago. That's one of the main benefits of the job. My apartment in Chicago is a month-to-month lease, and everything I own can fit into the back of my truck. There's nothing there that's really worth going back to, especially since Sadie's not there anymore."

Grace blinked down at him. "You'd…you'd consider moving to LA? For me?"

His smile was equal parts sweet and sinfully sexy, and it stirred her libido in a way she wouldn't have thought possible after everything they'd done during the night. "After last night? I'd consider moving to a dirt-floor hut in the outer reaches of fucking nowhere for you, angel."

He was heart-attack serious, Grace realized in amazement. He really *would* uproot his entire life to be with her. "Nick, we've known each other such a short amount of time. Is it crazy for us to be thinking like this?"

He reached down and grabbed her hand, lacing his fingers through hers. "Probably. But I don't really care. Look, as amazing as last night was, there's more to *this*—this connection between us—than just sex. I want to see where this goes. And there's no way we can do that if we're on opposite sides of the country. Do you feel the same?"

Grace bit her lip. "I do. But I feel like a really selfish bitch for letting you uproot your whole life so that we can, what, *date*?"

He leaned up and caught the lower lip she'd just bitten between his teeth, making her moan before letting go to whisper against her mouth, "I've never had anyone be selfish for me before. It's crazy hot."

She giggled. "You're just saying that because I'm naked, on top of you, and only recently finished giving you an early morning blow job."

He gave her ass a sharp swat with his free hand and grinned evilly when she yelped. "Always the argumentative lawyer, aren't you?"

"It's kind of my thing." Her smile slipped as she added, "I'm serious, though. I don't want you to do anything you'll regret."

He didn't miss a beat before saying, "The only thing I'd regret is letting you go without figuring out exactly what this thing is between us." He kissed her then, sending sparks through her entire body. "I need more time with you, and I'll do whatever it takes to get it."

Grace lost a few seconds of coherent thought as he traced the shell of her ear with his tongue, but in a sudden burst of clarity, the enormity of their conversation dawned on her and she jerked up.

"Holy shit," she squealed. "Did we just agree that you're moving to LA?"

He laughed. "So, you're OK with this?"

She shoved a hank of sweaty hair off her forehead and let her eyes rove over his face. He looked rumpled, sleepy-eyed, and gorgeous. And he was all hers. "Of course I am. I feel like I'm getting the better deal out of this."

"No way," he said quietly, pushing her hair behind her ears. "I'm a lucky man, angel."

Grace shot her best naughty smile as she rocked her hips against him. "Not yet, but I think you're going to get lucky again *very soon.*"

His eyes darkened a split second before he reversed their positions and flipped her onto her back. She let out an *oomph* that turned into a moan as he slid his tongue and lips down her neck, over her breasts, across her belly, then…lower.

"No," he whispered against her inner thigh. "I think it's *your* turn to get lucky again."

She wanted to protest that it wasn't her turn at all. In fact, if they were keeping score, she was ahead of him roughly three orgasms to one. But one long, hard stroke of his tongue through her wet folds obliterated that thought.

"Oh, God," she murmured, her thighs falling apart helplessly. "I guess it's my turn after all."

And ten minutes later, everyone on their floor heard just how lucky Grace was.

Chapter Twenty-eight

"So, is your name Nick, Jesus, God, or *Oh-My-God-Don't-Ever-Stop*? I'm confused because I heard you called a lot of things last night."

Grace stabbed her fork in Gage's direction and mumbled around a mouthful of pancakes, "Keep your mouth shut, Gage."

Nick just smirked and dove into his own breakfast, not looking the least bit embarrassed that half the hotel knew what they'd been doing all night. But then again, what did he have to be embarrassed about? From all the screaming she'd done, he came off looking like a sex god.

Which, now that she thought about it, wasn't at all far from the truth.

"Ugh," Gage muttered, reaching across Grace to grab the coffee decanter. "You have absolutely no shame. The fact that you're blushing so hard right now, Grace, just tells me you're replaying the whole thing in your head."

Grace took a sip of her orange juice before scoffing and saying, "I am not."

She totally was, though.

Grace lifted her eyes from her plate and found Nick pinning her with a look so hot and potent it let her know that he too was reliving their evening (and morning) in his head, right here at the breakfast table. One corner of his mouth lifted as their gazes held, and she had a brief fantasy about him throwing her down on the breakfast table and fucking her right there amid the pancakes and French toast and bacon platters.

So *sticky.*

She could honestly say that was the first sexual fantasy she'd ever had in a Cracker Barrel. Not sure if that was necessarily a *good* thing, but there was no denying it was kind of fun.

Gage grumbled, "Now you're just being smug about it. That kind of joy this early in the morning is just gratuitous, really."

"Jealous?" Nick asked mildly, snagging a piece of bacon off the plate in front of Grace. Seeing as he'd given her more orgasms than she'd ever had in her life over the course of one night, Grace decided she wouldn't stab Nick's hand with her fork for daring to touch her bacon. A lesser man would've been hospital-bound for fork-removal by now.

Gage glanced up as Sadie approached their table. "Totally," he said quietly, his eyes not leaving her face.

Sadie flushed a deep red, and shrugged out of her jacket, taking a seat next to Nick. "Sorry we're late," she said, slightly out of breath.

Michael came in behind her and threw himself down in the

chair next to Grace. "Pass the coffee and keep it coming," he muttered.

"Sure thing, princess," Gage said, shoving the decanter to Grace, who passed it over to Michael.

Michael glared at him. "Really? The princess thing again?"

He shrugged. "If the tiara fits."

Sadie quickly turned a giggle into a cough when Michael leveled her with a sharp glare. When she grabbed a plate and reached for the platter of pancakes, Michael cleared his throat pointedly and said, "I thought you were worried about fitting into that wedding dress."

Sadie drew her hand back from the platter as if it had scalded her. "Oh. Yeah. You're right. Maybe I'll just have some coffee, too," she said quietly.

Grace wanted to shake her. *No! Don't let anyone talk to you like that! Tell him to go fuck himself while you shovel pancakes down your throat, if that's what you want to do!*

And she wanted to smack her little brother upside the head. What was the matter with him? This wasn't the sweet kid she'd helped raise. When had Michael turned into such a monumental douchecanoe? Was it just the stress of the wedding that was causing him to turn into a groomzilla, or was there more to it than that?

Not that it really mattered at this point. She'd promised Nick she would stay out of Sadie and Michael's relationship. So, here she was, quietly (with gritted teeth) staying out of it.

And it really kind of sucked this time.

One look at Nick and she knew it sucked for him, too. He was looking at Michael with an expression only slightly friendlier than the one he usually gave Brad.

But Gage, who hadn't made any promises to stay out of anyone's business, swore under his breath and reached forward to stab a stack of pancakes with his fork. He dumped them on Sadie's plate without ceremony. "You should eat what you want. And a few pancakes today aren't going to keep you from fitting into a dress tomorrow." Then he jabbed his fork in Michael's direction and added, "And it's none of your damn business what anyone eats."

Michael's eyes narrowed on Gage. "It's not any of your business, either. *She's* not any of your business."

Well, well, Grace thought, it looked like her formerly clueless little brother was finally noticing that something weird was going on with Sadie and Gage. Good for him. But the breakfast table was hardly the place for such a discussion, so she tried to lighten the mood by saying, "I think I'm going to have T-shirts made up that say, 'It's none of your damn business what anyone eats.' I'd wear mine every time I went to a restaurant."

Nick grinned at her, but there was still tension in his eyes. He opened his mouth to say something to her, but whatever it was got swallowed whole by the sound of trinkets, wooden checkers sets, and jars of BBQ sauce hitting the floor in the little general store in front of the restaurant. The sounds of heated debate followed.

"What on earth is that all about?" Grace asked.

Gage raised a brow at her. "I'll give you three guesses," he began dryly, "and the first two don't count."

Right on cue, Ruthie rolled around the corner, looking fairly pleased with herself, with Brad behind her, pushing her wheelchair. Brad looked more embarrassed than Grace had ever seen him, which, childishly, brightened her mood considerably.

"Grace," Ruthie said as Brad parked her chair at the head of the table, "isn't it against the law to have an entryway in a public place that's so filled with crap you can't fit a wheelchair through?"

"I'm not helping you sue Cracker Barrel," Grace said with an eye roll.

Ruthie scowled at her. "Well, what good are you, then?"

"Ask Nick," Gage said mildly. "He knows what *good* Grace is."

Grace resisted the childish urge to flip him off, instead saying, "Who's a grumpy bastard?"

"Of course I'm a grumpy bastard. I didn't get any sleep last night."

"Technically, neither did I," Grace muttered.

"I didn't sleep either," Ruthie announced. "I heard *Wild Kingdom* noises all night."

Grace, who'd just taken a big drink, promptly spewed a mouthful of orange juice in Gage's direction.

"Are you fucking kidding me?" he grumbled, grabbing a stack of napkins to mop up the mess.

"Sorry," she choked out.

Not one to ever pick up on a social cue, Brad asked, "What do you mean by *Wild Kingdom* noises?"

Grace did a mental face-palm, but outwardly schooled her features into a mask of indifference, so as not to draw any more attention to herself, or to Nick, who looked altogether too pleased with himself.

"I mean *Wild Kingdom* noises," Ruthie repeated. "You know, like wild animals humping. Like a television special about horny monkeys."

Nick's smirk grew, and Grace leveled a scowl on him to let him know she was rethinking her earlier decision not to stab him with her fork.

"At least *someone* got lucky last night, because God knows *I* didn't," Michael groused quietly, which drew a sharp gasp from Sadie. Grace glanced over at Nick, who didn't seem to have heard Michael's comment. But Gage sure had, she noticed with no small amount of alarm.

An angry vein popped up in his forehead as Gage leaned forward in his seat, and in a low voice that Grace had never before heard him use, said, "Start showing her some god damned respect, asshole, or I'll drag you outside by the hair and beat the ever-lovin' fuck out of you."

Grace's breath caught. "Gage," she whispered.

Michael blinked at Gage like he'd never seen him before, but regained his composure quickly. Kind of.

His chair shrieked as Michael shoved away from the table. "I don't know what the *fuck* your problem is, man, but I'm over it." With that, he stood up and tossed a few bills on the table to cover the cost of the breakfast he'd barely touched. "I'm going back to the hotel."

When Sadie started to stand up, he waved her off. "Stay. I need some time alone anyway."

Then he was gone.

A full minute of tense silence passed. Nick reached over and give Sadie's hand a squeeze. "You okay?" he asked her.

She nodded, but still looked pale and shaky when she shifted her gaze to Gage. "That wasn't necessary," she said in a voice so quiet Grace had to strain to hear her. "The pancakes…saying that to him. You probably shouldn't have done it. But…thank you."

In the silence that followed, as Sadie and Gage locked eyes and seemed to get stuck that way, Brad cleared his throat and said, "Well, this has all been very awkward." Then he punctuated his statement with a nervous hyena giggle that made Grace cringe.

Ruthie sniffed. "No more awkward than you sitting here trying to win back a woman who was up all night making *Wild Kingdom* noises with an Irishman who probably goes through her purse while she's sleeping."

"Sometimes I don't even wait until she's asleep," Nick fired back without missing a beat. "Fill 'em up with sperm, then rob 'em blind while they search for their panties," he added in a dead-on Irish accent that would've done Colin Farrell proud. "It's the Irish way."

Grace practically had a snark-induced orgasm at that point. A snarkgasm. Had there ever been a more eloquently executed example of snark? It was *perfect.*

Grace had been falling in love with Nick for a while. But it was in that moment she realized she wasn't falling anymore. She'd already fallen. Anyone who could snark like Nick just had was a keeper.

Gage and Sadie stifled chuckles, while Ruthie *harrumphed* into her coffee cup, and Brad looked like he might have a stroke at any moment. Tossing his napkin to the table much like Michael had, Brad stood up and left, after announcing he needed some air.

"I hear the air is nice in Canada," Gage called after him. "You should go there to get some."

Grace couldn't agree more.

Ruthie, completely unfazed by Brad's departure, threw her hands up and said, "Where's the damn apple butter?"

Sadie handed Ruthie the apple butter while Grace silently thanked God that her parents had decided to skip breakfast. Having her dad hear about her sexcapades the previous night (and this morning) rated very low on her list of must-do's, somewhere between getting food poisoning again, and jabbing a fork in her eye.

"Is it too early to go somewhere and get drunk?" Nick asked, not really sounding like he was kidding.

"They really should serve vodka at family restaurants," Grace said. "When does anyone need a drink more than when they're with family?"

Gage nodded and added, "It's five o'clock somewhere."

Sadie smiled wanly at them. "I'm so sorry for ruining breakfast, everyone."

Nick opened his mouth to reply, but Gage beat him to the punch, saying, "You've got nothing to be sorry for. I'll talk with Michael. We'll get everything worked out."

Yeah, Grace thought, Gage, who was halfway in love with the bride-to-be, should have a chat with the groom-to-be. Good plan. "How about *I* talk to Michael after breakfast, so that Nick and Sadie can spend some time together?" *So that maybe, God willing, one of us can get to the bottom of whatever the fuck is going on with these two kids and this rushed, ill-advised wedding clusterfuck.*

"You know," Ruthie said as she smeared apple butter all over a biscuit, "Mavis Tarley in my book club says it's perfectly acceptable these days for girls to become lesbians. Not just ugly girls, either. Pretty ones like you can do it, too, Sadie. Just something to think about before you decide to marry into *this* family."

Everyone took a few moments of silence to digest *that* little nugget of crazy.

Chapter Twenty-nine

An hour and two pancakes—okay, *four* pancakes—later, Grace found Michael sulking all by himself in a lounge chair by the resort pool. She didn't bother with a greeting when she approached. She just smacked him on the back of his head with an open palm.

He yelped and shifted away from her. "What the fuck, Grace?"

She sat down, shaking her head. "I could ask you the same thing. And quit frowning at me like that. You know you deserved it. You were acting like a total douchenozzle at breakfast."

Michael shoved both hands through his already messy hair and groaned. "I know, I know. I knew it then, too, I just couldn't seem to stop it. I don't know what's wrong with me."

Maybe it's because you're a child getting ready to marry another child??? But instead of asking *that* aloud, Grace settled for, "Could it be nerves?"

He shrugged and picked at a loose string on a hole at the knee of his beaten-to-hell jeans. "I honestly don't know. Things between me and Sadie have been…different since we got here."

Grace took a slow, deep breath, knowing she was dangerously close to venturing into interference territory. If she was going to go there with Michael, she'd have to tread lightly. *Really* lightly. Like, sparrow-with-anorexia lightly.

"What do you mean *different*?" she asked carefully.

Michael blew out an exasperated breath. "Different, okay? We're usually completely in sync with one another, you know? We eat all the same foods, like all the same places, enjoy doing all the same things. We used to tell each other everything. And now, it's…I don't know. I'm finding out Sadie hasn't always told me the truth about her past, and she's letting Mom make all these wedding decisions for her." He paused, shaking his head again. "It's like…"

"You don't really know each other," Grace finished quietly.

"Yes," he answered, sounding relieved that she understood.

"You need to talk to her," Grace said. "Getting married is a huge deal, Michael. I'm sure you're both just…" *Jumping the gun on this thing? Far too young and naïve to even think about marriage? Acting like the stupid hormonal teenagers you are?* "…nervous and feeling the pressure, you know?"

He nodded. "I know you're right. But there's also this whole thing with Gage. I mean, after he helped her when she was sick, it's like there's…I don't know, this *bond* between them, or something. And then she started pulling away physically…I dunno. The whole thing is just starting to get really weird."

Danger, Will Robinson! You're about to interfere!

"Michael," she began gently, "do you still want to get married?"

Again with the shrug and eye-contact avoidance. "I love Sadie."

"Of course you do. She's awesome. But loving someone doesn't mean you have to marry them right away. Do you still want to marry her *now*?"

His eyes shifted to hers. "She wants a family. I love her, Grace. I want to give her everything she wants. I want her to be happy."

And that's exactly what Grace had been afraid of all along. Michael didn't care about getting married. He cared about Sadie and what it would take to make her happy. "You need to talk to her, Michael," Grace insisted. "Now. Get this all straightened out to determine if getting married tomorrow is still what you both want."

His eyes narrowed on her. "And if we decide it is? You'll stand by me and be my best man? Not lecture me or try to stop the wedding?"

She really didn't want to promise that. Grace was now more convinced than ever that getting married wasn't right for these two kids at the moment. Not that they couldn't eventually get their shit together and get it done, but by *tomorrow*? It just didn't seem prudent. Or likely. But with her promise to Nick hanging over her head like the sword of Damocles, she nodded and said with a conviction she didn't really feel, "Of course I'll stand by you. No lectures. I want you to be happy, Michael."

Even if what makes you happy now can emotionally devastate and ruin you a day, a month, or a year from now.

When Nick found Sadie, she was holding her wedding dress in front of her, staring into a full-length mirror in the reception hall as if answers to every question in the universe could be found in her own reflection. Nick didn't have much experience with such things, but if he had to guess, he'd say her expression was *not* that of an ecstatic woman about to be married the next day.

Sadie looked more like a woman about to go in for a pap smear.

"Hey, kid," he said, causing her to jump.

"Oh my God, Nick, you scared me."

She smiled at him, but Nick noticed it didn't quite reach her eyes. He sighed. He'd really been hoping he wouldn't have to have this conversation with his sister. But at this point, he didn't seem to have any other option. And since beating around the bush was also out of the question given their current time constraints, he asked, as gently as possible, "Having second thoughts?"

Her eyes widened for a split second before she burst out in a nervous, high-pitched laugh. "No way! Are you crazy? I have the dress, everything's been booked, Michael and I have been working three jobs to pay for everything, and everyone's here. The wedding *is* happening tomorrow."

Nick rubbed a hand over the back of his neck, feeling all kinds of awkward. "I'm not really asking if you're having second thoughts about the *wedding*, Sadie. I'm asking if you're having second thoughts about the *marriage*."

She blinked at him, then said, "I love Michael."

He nodded. "Of course you do. You wouldn't have said yes when he asked you to marry him if you didn't."

"Oh, he didn't ask me. I asked him."

"Well, sure you…wait, what?"

Sadie laughed again. "Don't look so shocked, Nick. It's 2018. A woman can ask a man to marry her, you know."

He was quiet for a moment while he processed what Sadie said. Of course a woman could ask a man to marry her, he thought. Nick wasn't a sexist. But this was *Sadie*. The girl who started writing stories about princesses and the princes who proposed to them when she was eight. The girl who kept a scrapbook full of wedding dress images under her pillow when she was fourteen. For *Sadie* to buck tradition and ask Michael to marry her? It was…weird. Absolutely nothing short of *weird*.

"And you didn't think…" Nick trailed off. *Jesus, maybe I should've let Grace handle this.* "…you were a little young to be making that kind of commitment? What was the hurry?" Then a horrible thought occurred to him. "Wait, you're not pregnant, are you?"

A blush tinged her cheeks, and she let out a disgusted snort. "No, Nick, I'm not pregnant. The birds-and-the-bees chat you had with me when I was nine stuck with me, okay?"

It had stuck with him, too. Shit. Was there anything worse than having to explain where babies came from to your little sister? He could still remember the intense relief he'd felt when she wrinkled up her little nose and said, "*Ew*, I'm never going to do *that*."

Ah, the good old days.

Sadie draped the wedding dress lovingly over the back of a velvet-covered chaise and tucked her arm through his. "Look, Nick, you're the one who taught me that when there's something I want, I should go after it hard, right?"

"Well, yeah."

"Well, I love Michael, and I can't really explain it, but it didn't take me long to realize I'm meant to be part of this family. I knew it as soon as I met his parents and Ruthie. And I figured, why wait, you know? So I made it happen. Just like you told me to do."

He frowned. "Babe, I remember that conversation, and I'm pretty sure I was talking about you getting picked for the swim team when you were twelve. I don't remember saying anything about getting *married*."

This time her laugh sounded genuine. "I know that. But the advice was still good." Her expression turned serious as she added, "I need this, Nick. Can you understand that?"

He understood better than anyone probably ever could. He'd done his best to take care of her when their family—which was really only a step above living on the streets to begin with—totally fell to shit. But for an impressionable little girl like Sadie, having a punk like him for a big brother could never compare to having a real family, like the one Grace and Michael had.

The kind of family Sadie was so obviously desperate to have.

What he'd told Grace had been right all along. He couldn't take this chance away from her. Sure, Michael had acted like a grade-A asshole this morning. But overall, it was pretty obvious the kid adored his sister. Michael was young and stupid, but he wasn't a bad guy. Sadie could do worse.

Nick sighed. "Alright, I'm only going to ask you one more thing, then I'll let it go and support whatever you decide, okay?"

When Sadie nodded, he asked, "Are you sure Michael's the one?"

Given how he'd seen her looking at Gage over the past couple of days, Nick thought the question was fair. He half expected Sadie to shoot back an indignant *of course*. But instead, she smiled wryly and asked, "Is anyone ever *really* sure? It's all a gamble, right? I mean, what does *the one* look like, anyway?"

Nick started speaking without really thinking. "*The one* is the first person you think about when you wake up, and the last before you go to bed. You feel like a part of you is missing when you're not with her, like you can't quite catch your breath until she's there at your side. You hear a funny joke and the first thing you want to do is call her, because you know she'll think it's funny, too. She's the one who holds your heart in her hands, and the idea doesn't even scare you because you trust her with it and know there's no one else on earth you'd ever want to give it to, anyway. She makes you want to be *better*. At everything. She's…the balance. Sunlight to darkness."

A few weeks ago, Nick wouldn't have had an answer to Sadie's question. So, now that the words had stopped flowing, he imagined he looked just as surprised at having said them as Sadie looked hearing them.

He was even more surprised that he'd meant every word.

Sadie's eyes filled with tears. "Wow," she whispered, voice thick with emotion. "Sounds like there's maybe someone you should be talking to more than me right now, Nicky."

I'm not looking for a relationship.

Yeah, but what would you do if you found one?

"Holy shit," he muttered as realization hauled off and slapped him across the face. "I love her."

Sadie grinned at him. "Ya think?"

He shoved both hands through his hair. "I can't tell her that. I've only known her for a week! She'll freak the fuck out!"

Sadie shrugged. "Maybe. But what if she doesn't? And who says love has a timetable, anyway? It's way too complicated for that."

Ugh. *Complicated.* Would that word ever *not* make him nauseous?

Chapter Thirty

After her talk with Michael, Grace decided to take the quickest route from the pool to her room, which unfortunately took her straight through the heart of the casino. Her eyes immediately teared up as she was smacked in the face with a wall of stale cigarette smoke.

Waving a hand in front of her in an attempt to clear the air, she squinted and tried to get her bearings. Between the smoke, the dim overhead lighting, and the rows of machines that flashed and alarmed obnoxiously, Grace was having a hard time even determining where the exit into the hotel was.

"Haven't seen you in here before, blondie. Hey, here's a nickel. Sit down here with me and try your luck."

Grace blinked at the woman who'd just pressed a nickel into her hand. From the scratchy, rough sound of her voice, Grace would've estimated the woman was Grandma Ruthie's age. But voices could certainly be deceiving, she quickly realized.

This woman looked like the love child of Snooki from *Jersey Shore* and Sharon Stone in *Casino.*

Grace imagined she was in her late fifties, though her impeccable makeup and trim figure (most of which was on display in a skin-tight, fuchsia tank dress) gave her a much more youthful appearance.

Smiling around a lit cigarette that was hanging precariously from her blood-red painted lower lip, the woman motioned for Grace to sit next to her at a slot machine that had a picture of a cartoon gangster from the 1920s on it.

"That machine went cold on me hours ago," the stranger said, "But maybe you'll have better luck."

"Oh, no thank you," Grace said. "I don't really gamble."

The woman laughed so hard she almost lost her cigarette. "I'm calling bullshit, honey. First of all, it's a nickel slot, not a high rollers' table in Atlantic City. It hardly counts as gambling. And secondly, I've seen you with my Nicky. You're a gambler, whether you recognize it or not."

Grace had been so distracted by the woman's raspy voice and teased platinum blonde, curls—which looked to be held in place with enough Aqua Net to supply Bon Jovi for a month in 1987—that she hadn't noticed the hint of a New Jersey accent in her words.

Grace took a seat at the gangster-themed slot machine and smiled. "You must be Nick's aunt, Lucille." She offered her a hand. "I'm Grace. It's very nice to meet you."

Lucille grabbed Grace's hand and gave it a firm squeeze before letting go to slip a nickel into her own slot machine. "You, too, sweetheart. Sorry I haven't made it to any of the family dinners. I guess I'm not what you'd call a people person," she said, making finger quotes around "people person".

She didn't sound particularly sorry, Grace noted. "I'm sure Nick and Sadie would've loved to have you there, but honestly, you didn't miss too much."

Just my family embarrassing themselves like usual.

Lucille snorted. "They wouldn't want me there. I was a shit aunt when they were kids. Nicky in particular never forgave me for it. Not that he should."

Well, this had certainly taken an awkward turn rather quickly. "Well, um, I'm sure you did the best you could."

Her lip curled up on one side. "You're adorable. It's no wonder Nicky loves you so much."

Warmth spread through Grace's entire body at the thought of Nick loving her, but she quickly squelched it. Just because she was batshit crazy over him didn't mean the insanity was mutual. Sure, he wanted to see how their relationship would progress, but love? Not likely after such a short amount of time. So, Grace kept her mouth shut. Lucille, though? Not so much.

"I was young when my sister went to prison," she said, not even looking at Grace as she fed her slot machine and pulled the lever. "Immature, too. Not the kind of woman anyone should trust to raise a couple of kids, you know? But too bad for them I was all they had. Maybe I was better than foster care, but probably not by much."

Grace's stomach churned. Poor Nick and Sadie. Orphaned, taken in by a woman who admittedly wasn't mother material. How awful it must've been for them.

"We didn't have much of anything," Lucille went on. "I worked all the damn time trying to keep the bills paid and clothes on those kids' backs. And that's all Nicky ever really needed from me." She shook her head, smiling to herself. "He was such an arrogant little punk." She huffed out a laugh. "Didn't need nothin' from nobody. Always the tough guy. But Sadie always wanted more. More love, more attention. She was real needy, you know? But, me not being a people person and all, I never gave her what she needed."

Grace heard the regret in Lucille's voice and felt a stab of empathy. If she'd been in the same situation, if she'd been forced into a parental role now, could she do any better than Lucille had done? Grace wasn't sure.

Lucille cleared her throat. "Don't get me wrong. I gave Sadie what she needed to stay *alive*, but Nicky's the one who gave her what she *needed*. He raised her. Loved her. Taught her how to be a good person. I was a shitty, selfish excuse for a mother figure, but Nicky…he'd do anything to make her happy. Even somethin' that wasn't in her best interest."

Grace frowned. "What do you mean by that?"

Lucille swiveled on her chair and looked down her nose at Grace. "I mean he'd let her marry your brother even though it's the most fucked-up idea in the history of fucked-up ideas."

Grace wasn't sure who she should stand up for first: her brother, Nick, or Sadie. "Well, honestly, it's not our business. This is between Sadie and Michael."

The look Lucille pinned her with was entirely too knowing for Grace's peace of mind. "That's Nicky talking. I can tell you would've intervened by now if it'd been up to you. You're following his lead, and I can respect that. But don't pretend it's the way you would've handled things."

No, Grace thought, going with the flow was definitely *not* how she usually handled things. That was all thanks to Nick. But she couldn't exactly say he was wrong. There was some obvious merit to letting Sadie and Michael work out their problems on their own.

"Look," Lucille said, "I'm not one to beat around the bush, blondie…"

Understatement of the year.

"…and I think you would agree with me that this marriage is a shit idea. Not that I think there's anything wrong with your brother. He's a cute kid. Seems nice enough. But he's young. Way too young to get married."

"Well, yes, but—"

"And Sadie's too young to make a commitment like that. If she wasn't, she wouldn't be making puppy-dog eyes at your cousin—who, by the way, is hot as the devil himself. I made a solid pass at him in the hotel bar the other night, and he turned me down cold. Guess he isn't into cougars." Lucille paused to hike up the top of her tank dress. "His loss. But anyhow, it's up to you to be the voice of reason here, Grace. You're going to have to talk Michael into walking away from Sadie tomorrow, because she won't be strong enough to walk away on her own."

Grace was at a loss. First of all, how did Lucille, who hadn't spent one minute with the family so far since their arrival, know so much about what was going on with everyone? Did she have spies in the hotel or something? She must've.

Second, even though she sort of secretly agreed with Lucille, doing anything to interfere with the wedding would be breaking her word to Nick, and there was no way she could do that. She'd never be able to betray him like that. He meant way too much to her.

Third…Lucille made a pass at Gage? *Ew*!

She shook her head. "It's not up to me, Lucille. If you have something to say to Sadie about her marriage, it's up to you to say it, not me. I made a promise to Nick that I would stay out of this and let the kids work things out on their own. I'm not going back on my word to him."

Grace didn't *actually* stomp her foot to make her point, but in her head she did.

Lucille studied her with a steely-eyed stare that up until that point, Grace had only ever seen Detective Reagan give perps on *Blue Bloods*. It was like she was looking straight into Grace's *soul.* It was terribly unnerving. But after a long moment, Lucille broke out a wide smile that somehow made Grace even more nervous.

"Thanks, blondie. That's exactly what I wanted to hear. I guess you'll do, after all."

Grace considered herself to be an intelligent person. She was hardly ever at a loss for words. But still, she heard herself muttering, "Huh?"

Lucille pulled the lever on her slot machine with relish. "I was hopin' you'd tell me to go to hell when I asked you to interfere in the wedding, and you did, in your own lawyerly kind of way. Kudos, doll."

Grace was still confused. "You mean you *didn't* really want me to talk Michael out of marrying Sadie?"

Lucille chuckled. "Fuck, no. That'd piss Nicky off something fierce. But I had to know if the girl he's in love with had some integrity and loyalty. You bein' a lawyer and all, you can see why I was concerned."

The lawyer comment barely phased her. Nobody really liked lawyers. Until they needed one, that is. But the *girl he's in love with* part really stuck with her. Was it possible? Could Nick really be in love with her? How would Lucille know if he was?

She quickly kneecapped that thought before it could take root. Speculation was less than worthless, in her professional (and personal) experience. "You played me," Grace murmured.

"Like a harp from hell, doll."

There wasn't an ounce of guilt in her voice, either. Then something occurred to Grace. "Why would someone who is a shitty, selfish excuse for a mother figure care about what kind of person Nick may or may not be in love with?"

One of Lucille's perfectly painted-on eyebrows raised incredulously. "You really are a lawyer, aren't ya?"

Grace raised a brow at her in return.

Lucille smiled again. "Just because I'm not cut out to be a mother doesn't mean I don't love those kids like they were my own."

Grace chewed on that one for a moment before saying, "You know, it's never too late to be there for Nick and Sadie."

Lucille looked downright wistful for a moment, but then she blinked and the look was gone. She sniffed. "We'll see. But I feel better knowing you'll be there for Nicky when the whole thing falls apart tomorrow."

"Of course I…wait, what?"

Lucille rolled her eyes. "Oh, come on. We both know that wedding ain't happening. Those kids are breaking up tomorrow, even if you don't do the breaking yourself."

"What makes you so sure?"

"You're not a gambler, but I am, and I win more than I lose. Why? Because I make more safe bets than risky ones." She fed another nickel into her slot machine. "And a breakup tomorrow? That's a safe bet."

Grace opened her mouth to argue, but snapped it shut again, fearing that anything she said would lead her directly into another one of Lucille's word snares. So instead, she muttered a few *nice-to-meet-you's* and *hope-to-see-you-again-soon's* before getting up to leave the casino.

She'd only made it a few steps before Lucille called out to her.

"Oh, blondie? Just so you know, if you do end up hurting or betraying Nicky? I have people on speed dial who can make bodies disappear for a few hundred bucks, a case of PBR, and a bag of lye. Just so you know. Are we clear?"

Grace looked for some sign in Lucille's eyes that she was kidding. After finding none, she nodded and muttered another goodbye.

Jesus, she thought when she made her way back into the

hotel. And she'd thought *her* family was complicated.

Chapter Thirty-one

The sun shone brighter than usual the next day. The flowers in the vase by the bed in her room smelled a little sweeter. Colors looked a little more vibrant. It was a beautiful, beautiful day.

Or maybe everything was no different than it was yesterday and all of that was just a pleasant side effect of two full nights—*in a row*—of sweaty, athletic, mind-blowing sex and so many orgasms Grace had lost count.

Whatever the reason, it was a *glorious* day…even though Grace had almost managed to make a complete *ass* of herself with Nick the night before.

She'd almost said that *thing*. That *thing* a woman should never say to a man when he was inside her. That thing that made so many men run for the hills. The memories of her almost-epic failure assailed her against her will.

He cupped her face in his hands and stared down into her eyes as he slowly—so, so slowly—slid into her, inch by hot, hard inch. "You're amazing," he said on a ragged groan.

She blinked back tears at the reverence, the awe, in his eyes as he looked down at her. "Oh, God, Nick, I love…"

He stopped moving, his gaze intensifying. "You what?" he asked.

Grace felt a blush rising to her cheeks as she panicked.

She'd almost told him she loved him.

She knew Nick had feelings for her. She knew he wanted her. He wouldn't be willing to move to LA to date her if he didn't. But love? It was too soon for that!

Even though she was 100% sure love was exactly what she felt for him.

When she stubbornly bit down on her lower lip and remained silent, he pulled back, almost pulling completely out of her. "You what?" he prodded.

Her mind raced. Well, as much as it could race with him overwhelming her senses like he was. The best way to avoid honestly answering a direct question was to offer up an alternative response that was still true, she realized.

And reminding a man that she had breasts couldn't hurt, either.

So, instead of blurting out that she loved him, Grace arched her back, which shoved her breasts into his chest, making him groan aloud, and said, "I love this. How you feel in me. God, I just want you so much. I've never wanted anyone the way I want you."

It had worked, too. To an extent, at least. Grace could tell Nick hadn't believed that was what she'd intended to say, but apparently her absolutely true statement had been sufficient, because he'd plunged back into her immediately.

And the best part? He'd maintained eye contact with her the entire time they'd made love. Every time they'd made love, as a matter of fact. No closed eyes, no dropping his head to her shoulder, no glancing down at her breasts, no weird *O* face. He'd held her gaze the whole time as if he wanted nothing more in the world than to watch her come. It was intense and erotic in a way sex had never been for her before. Maybe because with Nick, it wasn't *just* sex.

Grace silently did the math on when she'd be able to tell Nick she loved him without him thinking she was crazy. Maybe when they were in LA? Certainly not before. But then again, math had never been her strong suit. Maybe she should just…

"Boy, what in the hell is the matter with you? Are you constipated?"

And so much for mental math, Grace thought, as every calculation fled in the wake of Ruthie's words, bringing her back at jarring speeds to the here and now, which was the small room next to the reception hall that had been designated as the groom-to-be's ready room.

Michael straightened his tie and blew out a harsh breath. "I'm fine, Grandma."

Ruthie patted the cloud of blue curls Grace had spent an hour arranging for her, then started digging through her handbag. "You don't look fine. I have a supplement in here that could get you going in no time. You don't want to be all bound up on your wedding night."

Sarah brushed a wrinkle out of her silk skirt and frowned at

Michael. "Don't take anything she pulls out of her purse. You'll wake up the next day with no memory of what happened and suspicious wheel marks across your back."

Ruthie rolled her eyes. "It's not my fault you can't hold your sedatives."

"You told me it was aspirin," Sarah said dryly.

"An honest mistake," Ruthie said, and sniffed.

"And the fact that you tried to drive over me in your chair while I was passed out on the ground?"

Another sniff. "I might've panicked while trying to get help."

Sarah's jaw dropped. "You didn't get help! You let me lie there for four hours! You didn't even—"

Michael shoved his hands through his hair and growled—honest to God *growled*—like a pissed-off Rottweiler. "Get out!"

Everyone jumped, but it was Grace who found her voice first. "Okay. We'll go. Sorry about that."

Michael grabbed her arm. "Not you. Everyone *but* you. Get out."

"Michael Thomas Montgomery," Sarah whispered, aghast. "What in the h-e-double-hockey-sticks has gotten into you?"

He looked so lost in that moment that Grace's heart broke

for him. She took her mother's arm and led her to the door. "I'm sure it's just pre-wedding jitters, Mom," she said. "Nothing to worry about. Why don't you go check in with Gage and dad and make sure everything looks good in the reception hall, okay?"

Sarah somewhat reluctantly nodded her agreement, and moved aside to let Ruthie roll by on her way out the door.

"See?" Ruthie said to Sarah as they both left. "I told you the boy's constipated. No one's that grumpy when they're regular."

When they were gone, Grace threw her hands up in the universal what-the-hell gesture. "Talk to me."

Michael closed his eyes, took a deep breath, then blurted, "Sadiecriedduringsexlastnight."

Grace had a quick mind, but that was a little too quick even for her. "Pardon?"

"Sadie. Cried. During. Sex. Last. Night," he said through gritted teeth.

She blinked at him. "She Meredith Grey'ed you?"

"What?"

"Season two, Grey's Anatomy, Meredith cried during sex with…oh, never mind." Grace shook her head. "I guess that's not important. You're going to have to back up and tell me the whole story."

Much to my dismay, she thought. The thought of hearing about her brother's sex life had her choking back a little vomit, but damn it, she was the best man at this wedding. It was her job to put Michael's mind at ease. Even if his fiancée was crying during sex.

Yikes.

She listened patiently—doing her level best to maintain a completely impartial expression—as Michael told her about the conversation he'd had with Sadie the night before. How they'd both opened up and talked about how much they loved each other.

"She's my best friend," Michael said, chewing on his thumbnail like he used to when he was a little boy afraid to get a shot at the pediatrician's office. "I'm *her* best friend. So, I asked her if she still wanted to go through with the wedding. She said she did. I thought everything was fine. So, we started…you know…"

Oh, God.

"…and right before I, uh, you know…"

Grace pressed her hands to her stomach. *Don't puke. Don't puke. Don't puke.*

Michael looked equally miserable as he said, "I looked down at her face, her eyes met mine, and I smiled. I thought she'd smile back, but…"

"She started crying instead," Grace murmured.

He nodded, grimacing. "And not like a few happy tears, either. We're talking gut-wrenching, someone-just-killed-her-puppy *sobs*. It was *awful*. I didn't know what to do. I just kind of awkwardly held her and whispered over and over again that she was going to be okay, that I was there for her. She eventually fell asleep, and when I woke up this morning she was gone. Nick told me she was in her ready room getting dressed hours ago."

Grace shook her head, stunned. "And you're sure you didn't say anything to upset her? You didn't let Grandma Ruthie talk to her or anything, did you?"

He looked offended at the mere suggestion. "Fuck, no. We purposefully avoided everyone last night. We didn't fight or anything. It was just a conversation and sex. I didn't do anything wrong, Grace, I swear!"

Grace rubbed her now-aching temples. Jesus. What a mess. Could Lucille have said something to upset Sadie? But as soon as the thought entered her mind, Grace dismissed it. Lucille had seemed willing to let the wedding play out if Grace wasn't going to do her bidding and step in to stop it. She also didn't strike Grace as the kind of person who would toy with her niece's emotions for fun, either.

Why was it that Meredith had cried during sex with George on *Grey's Anatomy*? Grace tried to remember, but the answer must have been lodged somewhere towards the back of Grace's brain, most likely buried under various legal precedents, copious amounts of random song lyrics, and useless *Star Wars* trivia, because she couldn't quite put her finger on it at the moment.

Seriously, how could she remember every word of REM's *It's the End of the World as We Know It*, but not be able to call up a major plotline from a show she'd been watching for a million seasons? *Ugh.* So frustrating.

With a sigh, Grace gave up trying to recall that stupid episode that probably had nothing to do with Sadie's crying jag the previous night, anyway. "I'll go talk to Nick, okay? We'll see if she said anything to him."

Michael looked so relieved that Grace's heart hurt for him. He shoved a hand through his already-disheveled hair and offered her a weak smile. "Thanks, Gracie. I owe you for this. Big time."

And as she was walking out the door, it hit her.

The reason Meredith cried while having sex with George was that she was really in love with Derek, but couldn't have him. George was a placeholder, and she felt awful about it.

Oh…just…hell.

Grace turned the corner out of the groom's ready room and face-planted with an *oomph* into a heavenly scented wall of man chest.

Nick put his hands on her waist to steady her. "Whoa. Sorry.

I…uh…"

She smiled up at his befuddled expression. "You, uh, what?"

He stepped back and rubbed a hand over his furrowed brow before muttering, "I've never been turned on by anyone wearing a tux before. This is weird. Give me a second, will you?"

She couldn't hold back a giggle as she glanced down at her crisp black tux, glaring-white dress shirt, and sky-high, black, fuck-me Manolo Blahniks. "It's not too much? I thought it'd be appropriate since I'm the best man. My assistant had the guy who works on all my business suits in LA tailor it and overnight it. I'm pretty sure he thought I was nuts, but I think he did a good job anyway, right?"

Nick slid a finger into the collar of his own crisp white dress shirt and pulled it away from his skin like it was choking him. "You look amazing, Grace. The guy did better than *good.* I'm thinking I should send him a thank-you note or something."

Before she could respond, he bent down and captured her mouth in a kiss that told her just exactly *how* amazing he thought she looked in her tux.

When she pulled back, eyes most likely glazed with lust, brain at least partially melted, she licked her lips and said, "Yeah…maybe I should send him a thank-you note, too. Along with a nice fruit basket or something?"

His chuckle sounded like rough sex and dirty talk, and it did naughty, naughty things to her. "Where were you rushing off to?" he asked.

Grace kneecapped her wayward hormones and refocused on the problem at hand. "Michael was worried about Sadie. I was going to check and make sure everything is okay. Have you talked to her?"

His expression turned serious enough that it effectively squashed any remaining dirty thoughts Grace might've had. There was definitely trouble in paradise.

"She's, uh, not really talking," Nick said. "She's in her ready room, all dressed and everything, just staring into the mirror. That's actually why I was coming to find you. Do you think you could check on her? Make sure she doesn't need anything?"

The mother of all bad feelings washed over Grace. The Khaleesi of bad feelings. The kind of bad feeling that other bad feelings aspired to be when they grew up.

This couldn't possibly end well.

But looking into Nick's hopeful face, remembering Michael's hopeful face, Grace gave the only answer she could.

"Of course I'll talk to her." She swallowed the lump of foreboding that wedged itself into her throat and studiously ignored the *Star Trek* red alert siren blaring in her brain. "I'm sure she's just working through some last-minute jitters."

Or some last-minute second thoughts caused by her attraction to the groom's cousin, the little devil on Grace's shoulder muttered.

Suck it up and do whatever you can to help, the little angel on Grace's other shoulder replied.

Squaring both shoulders and taking a deep breath, Grace gave Nick what she hoped was a comforting smile and turned away. But he stopped her by grabbing the hand she'd raised to knock on Sadie's door. "Grace, I, uh, I wasn't only coming to find you to talk to Sadie for me. I also wanted to tell you that I, uh…well, that is to say that I…"

She frowned up at him. Wow, he suddenly really looked awful. Kind of sweaty and nervous. Maybe a little nauseous. And his hand was clammy. Nick wasn't the kind of guy who was ever clammy. "What's wrong?"

He opened his mouth and it looked like he wanted to say something, but no words escaped. It felt kind of like she was standing in front of Edvard Munch's *The Scream*. Grace tightened her grip on his clammy hand and said, "Okay, now you're scaring me. What's going on, Nick? What did you need to tell me?"

Instead of answering, he kissed her again. And this kiss was…different than any they'd ever shared. Usually, their kisses were all clashing tongues and teeth, dripping in need, like they were trying to crawl inside each other because that was the only way they'd ever get close enough. But this kiss was slow, deep, sensual. He was trying to tell her something with this kiss—something he couldn't find the words to express.

Grace had no idea what he was trying to say, but she liked it. A lot.

Finally, when they broke apart, gasping for breath, Nick laid his forehead against hers. A muscle in his jaw jumped, letting Grace know Nick still had something else to say. But the way their last kissing-in-lieu-of-actual-words experiment had gone, Grace wasn't sure she could afford to let him express himself again. As a lawyer, she didn't think an indecent exposure charge would exactly *help* her career in any way.

She gave him one last kiss—a super-quick one, lest she get sucked into his sexual vortex again—before pulling away and offering him another smile. "We'll talk later?"

He huffed out an exasperated breath and shoved a hand through his hair before giving her a terse nod. "Yeah. Later."

If she only had the terrified look on his face to go by, Grace wasn't sure talking was a good idea at all. But the way her luck was running today, she could bet that whatever Nick's problem was, it was *complicated.*

Chapter Thirty-two

"Ladies' golf is manlier than what I just saw you do, boy."

Nick looked over, then down—way, way down—to find the source of the disgusted, three-packs-a-day voice. "Lovely to see you, too, Ruthie," he managed to spit out through gritted teeth.

She sniffed and adjusted the wilted corsage that was pinned to the lapel of her cotton-candy pink dress suit. The color of the dress in combination with her blue curls and the oddly shaped, eggplant-colored hat she wore was jarring. The old lady looked a little like the circus had puked all over her.

Ruthie sat up straighter in her wheelchair and frowned at him. "You know, I was married to my Earl for forty-two years. He died years ago. Massive heart attack."

If this was a tell-the-people-you-love-that-you-love-them-before-they-up-and-die-on-you speech, Nick didn't really want to hear it. He knew he'd wussed out just now when he'd tried to tell Grace he loved her. He knew he still needed to tell her. And he would. Eventually.

Just as soon as he could seem to force the words past his uncooperative tongue, which for some reason, went into a coma when he was trying to say "I love you" to Grace.

He'd tried to tell her. He truly had. But it wasn't as easy as people in romantic comedies made it look. Nick had never told anyone he loved them, other than his sister, of course. Those words…they weren't just *words* to him. He knew he *felt* them, but voicing them was an entirely different animal.

That's when he noticed Ruthie was still looking up at him expectantly. "I'm sorry for your loss," Nick murmured when it became apparent that the old woman had no intention of going away anytime soon.

She snorted. "There was no loss. He was a total bastard. A mean drunk who beat me every chance he got and a gambler who lost most of our life savings at the craps tables in Atlantic City. If it weren't for my bad back, I would've done a jig of pure glee on that old fucker's grave when he finally kicked. If there's any justice in this world, he's roasting on a spit in hell right now."

Well, that was a bit of a conversation stopper, now wasn't it? Nick had no idea how to respond, so…he didn't.

"Oh, I know what you're thinking," she went on. "You're thinking I'm exaggerating, or that maybe he was only horrible because I'm such a bitter old hag."

If the shoe fits…

Her lip curled as she stared up at him. "*That's* where you're supposed to disagree and say something nice about me, Irish. I thought your people at least had *charm* going for them."

His brain panicked again for a second, groping for something nice to say about Ruthie and coming up black-hole empty. Literally *nothing* nice came to mind. She was mean and spiteful and bigoted. She also seemed to take pleasure—giddy joy, really—in the suffering of others. Nope. He had nothing.

Ruthie rolled her eyes. "Don't hurt yourself there, pretty boy. No need to try and *think*. I can practically smell the burning rubber. I know I'm not exactly a ray of sunshine, but that wasn't always the case. I was a good wife. Just the kind of wife Earl wanted. Soft-spoken. Always had dinner on the table at six when he got home. Accepted his apology gracefully when he knocked me down two flights of stairs because I'd forgotten to pick up his dry cleaning."

Great. Now he was pissed at himself for failing to tell Grace how he felt *and* hating himself for not being able to offer Ruthie any kind words. "I'm sorry you had to go through that, ma'am."

She leaned forward and swatted him in the stomach with the back of her hand. "Aren't you listening at all? I'm not sorry I had to go through that! Going through all that made me who I am today. And who I am today is an old lady who wouldn't ever let a man treat her like dirt again. I'm an old lady who says exactly what she wants whenever she wants. When I hate someone, I tell 'em. And when I love someone, well, that doesn't happen as often, but I tell 'em that, too. You won't find me falling apart, sweating like a pig, unable to say 'I love you' to the best thing I'll ever find in my lifetime. Life's too short for that shit."

Nick blinked down at her, pretty sure that was the most he'd ever heard her say, and there hadn't been a single racist or sexist comment in the whole speech. "Well, thank you, Ruthie. That was…inspiring." Kind of. "When I see Grace next, I'll try to be more like you. I'll tell her how I feel."

Ruthie looked him up and down, and apparently decided she didn't like what she saw, because her face pinched up like she'd just taken a giant swig of vinegar. "I don't know why I bother. I'm sure you'll screw it all up somehow. The pretty ones are always so, so dumb," she muttered.

Nick manfully stifled a shriek when she wheeled her chair right over his toes. He forced himself to stand up straight and not hop up and down on his good foot to avoid putting weight on the one she'd just crushed when she glanced back at him over her shoulder.

"You know," she began conversationally, "I do a lot of reading in my spare time. I ran out of Grisham and Koontz books one time years ago, so I started reading all of Gage's journals and texts from med school. It's a little scary how easy it is to cause an otherwise healthy man to have a massive heart attack." Her gaze sharpened to the point that Nick could practically feel it pricking his skin. Then she added, "I just thought you'd find that interesting."

Wait…what?

Nick was pretty sure he looked like a confused puppy as he

tipped his head to one side and stared down at her. "Are you saying…"

"I'm saying that Grace is one of mine. I take care of what's mine. Do right by her, and tread lightly, Irish. Don't make me hurt you."

And with an evil cackle the likes of which Nick hadn't heard since he'd watched *The Wizard of Oz* with Sadie when they were just kids, Ruthie was gone.

His mind was spinning like a drunk on a Tilt-a-Whirl. So, so many questions, so few answers.

What was going on with his sister? How was he going to find the words to tell Grace he loved her? What was *Grace* feeling? Was she really over her divorce? Was it possible that she could love him, too?

Did Ruthie kill Earl?

All he knew for sure was that he didn't have to worry about complicating his life anymore. Surely this was as complicated as it was going to get.

Right?

Chapter Thirty-three

Sadie stood in a puddle of buttery sunlight in front of the full-length mirror in the bride's ready room, looking pale and terrified and magnificent in her borrowed wedding dress.

She somehow managed to look rooted to the floor and ready to bolt all at the same time. Grace approached her calmly, slowly, just like she'd approach a scared baby bird. Sadie looked that fragile, that *broken*.

A thousand swear words ran through Grace's mind, but she swallowed them down. She'd seen this look before. Mostly in the eyes of clients who were about to get audited by the IRS or raked over the coals by a board of investors.

"Sadie," she said in near-whisper. "Is everything OK?"

There was a pause so long that Grace contemplated repeating the question before Sadie blurted, "I don't even know how I like my steak."

Well, that wasn't at *all* what Grace had expected her to say. But food was a good, tangible problem that Grace could fix, so she latched onto it. "Are you hungry? Do you want me to get you a steak?"

Sadie whirled away from the mirror so fast Grace stumbled back a step. "You don't get it," Sadie began, her voice high and thready in a way that made Grace even more nervous, "I. Don't.

Know. How. I Like. My. Steak."

Grace opened and closed her mouth a few times as she searched for the correct response. But after a moment of coming up blank, she just shook her head, shrugged her shoulders, and said, "I'm going to need more information, Sadie. What does steak have to do with…" she paused, gesturing to Sadie's state of wide-eyed panic, "…all this?"

Sadie whirled back to the mirror and shoved both hands into her hair, causing Grace to gasp in horror. It had taken her mother two hours to create the intricate up do Sadie was sporting, and she'd just ruined it with one gesture. Somehow she just knew her mom would blame her instead of Sadie for the lost hours.

"At breakfast this morning, I ordered steak and eggs, because when I was sick, Gage said I was underweight and needed more protein in my diet. The waiter asked how I wanted my steak cooked. I couldn't answer him, Grace. Do you understand what I'm saying?"

No. Not even close. But she guessed, "Of course I do. How you cook a steak is really important to the flavor. I mean, well-done is best from a food safety standpoint, but it can get really dry that way. Medium-rare is tender, but not everyone can handle seeing the red in their meat. It's…not an easy decision. That could've happened to anyone."

Inwardly, Grace groaned. Wow, she was really bad at comforting people. Why was she rambling about steak, for God's sake? She should've sent her mom in to talk to Sadie. No way would her mom go on a lengthy rant about steak at a time like this.

Sadie shook her head as her eyes welled with tears. "No, you don't get it. I couldn't answer because I always just order whatever Michael's having, and Michael wasn't with me. I can't make decisions on my own, Grace. Not even easy ones like how I want a damn steak cooked. He's my only friend. That's why I don't even have bridesmaids, for God's sake. I take the same classes he takes. I go where he goes, like what he likes." Tears mixed with mascara carved a path down the flawless finish of her makeup. "I live his *life*. I don't even know who I am when I'm not with him."

Suddenly Grace wanted to get her little brother in a headlock and beat the crap out of him. "Sadie, Michael shouldn't have made you feel like that. Relationships are about compromise. He doesn't get to always win. You need to talk—"

"No," Sadie interrupted. "It's not his fault. He would've compromised. I just never asked him to. I wanted to be a part of your family so bad, Grace. I think I wanted to be part of your family more than I wanted…"

She trailed off, but Grace knew what she meant.

She'd wanted to be part of the family more than she'd actually wanted *Michael*. She'd turned herself into a perfect little Montgomery family fembot without even realizing it, just to fit in with the family she'd never had.

Oh boy. This was even worse than Grace had thought.

Grace swallowed hard. "Maybe you two just need to slow down. I mean, you love each other, right?"

She hesitated, but she nodded.

"And you're *in* love with each other…right?" Grace prompted.

There was no nod this time, only a panicked, wild-eyed stare, and Grace's heart plummeted to her shoes. "Oh, Sadie," she said on a deep sigh.

The quiet tears gave way to gut-wrenching sobs. "I know I'm a horrible person," she said in between gasps for air, "but I really did think I was in love with him until Nick told me what finding *the one* was supposed to feel like. I love Michael, but I don't love him the way Nick loves you."

Grace took the words like a punch to the gut. Nick loved her back? Lucille hadn't been imagining it? He *loved* her? Like 'til-death-do-you-part, let's-adopt-a-dog-together, here-you-can-have-the-last-brownie kind of *love*? And he'd told his *sister* instead of telling her? She'd been stressing out, doing the mental math on when she'd be able to tell him how she felt, and he'd been keeping *this* from her? What the hell?

Then she remembered Nick had been trying to tell her something before she came to talk to Sadie. Something that made him look like he wanted to vomit.

"Oh my God," she whispered. Could it really be true?

"The things he said about you…I've never felt that way for anyone," Sadie choked out. "The closest I've come to feeling like *that* is with…"

That sentence fragment snapped Grace out of her *Holy-Mother-of-Jesus-Nick-loves-me-back* stupor real quick. "Gage," Grace finished for her.

Sadie gave her a weak, watery smile. "No one has ever taken care of me before except for Nick."

Grace rubbed her aching temples. This was sooooooo much information. And it was all so messy. Yikes. "Well, he's a doctor, so of course he took care of you," she said reasonably. She said it reasonably because that was a really *reasonable* explanation. Reasonable beat *this-is-a-clusterfuck-of-epic-proportions* every time, right?

Sadie's answering expression told Grace that reasonable was not a factor here. Apparently they were going to go with the clusterfuck. *Gah*!

Work with me here, Sadie. Work with me!

"It's more than that," Sadie finally said. "I can *feel* Gage in a room even when I can't see him. I know when he's watching me, even though he turns away before I can catch him doing it. Have you ever felt like that before?"

"Yes," Grace murmured, thinking immediately of Nick. If he was anywhere within a mile of her, her body seemed to realize it and react accordingly. Hell, her nipples were on high alert right now because she knew he was a few rooms away, waiting on her to get back from checking on his sister.

"Michael's my best friend and I'll always love him. But I wouldn't feel this connection with Gage if what I had with Michael was *forever*, would I?" Sadie asked quietly.

Grace swallowed hard. She wouldn't touch that question with a twenty-foot pole. But the implications were clear. Poor Michael. "What do you want to do, Sadie? What can I do to help?"

Wiping her tears with the back of her hand, Sadie straightened to her full height. "Look, nothing is going to happen with Gage. I'm too messed up right now to even think about that, and I wouldn't do that to your family. But I *do* need help, Grace. And you're not going to like it, but I'm going to ask anyway."

Grace's heart dropped into the pointy toes of her Manolos. "On a scale of one to ten, one being cauliflower, five being sitting front row at a Jon Mayer concert, and ten being—oh, I don't know—clubbing baby seals, how much am I going to hate what you want me to do?"

Sadie's watery chuckle echoed through the room, but the look in her eyes was anything but encouraging.

Grace's chin hit her chest. "*Ugh.* Ten it is."

Let's go club some baby seals.

Chapter Thirty-four

About a hundred years later, Grace emerged from the bride's ready room and made her way into the reception hall, looking worn out and…something Nick couldn't quite place. Guilty, maybe?

Shit. That couldn't possibly be good, now could it?

Everyone rushed her at once. Michael wanted to know if Sadie was okay. Gage—who smelled like a distillery and looked like something that had been scraped off the bottom of an old sneaker—wanted to know where Sadie was. Sarah wanted to know if the dress fit. David wanted to know if Grace had remembered to pack an extra Kindle charger, because his wasn't working. Ruthie wanted to know if the reception was going to include an open bar.

Nick just wanted to know why Grace was ignoring everyone else and looking at him like she was very sorry, but that she was going to have to stab him through the heart with one of her stilettos.

Grace held up a hand and told everyone to wait for a minute while she pulled Michael aside. Nick couldn't hear what they were saying, but watching as Grace spoke to her brother at a frantic pace, and seeing Michael's expression shift through the five stages of grief in under five minutes, he knew the wedding wasn't happening.

Son of a bitch. Sadie wouldn't recover from this.

Nick refused to stay out of the conversation any longer. Stalking over to where Grace and Michael were huddled behind a giant spray of roses and lilies, he grabbed her arm, forcing her to meet his gaze. "Where's my sister?"

Grace swallowed hard. "She left, Nick. She couldn't go through with the wedding, and she was too embarrassed to face anyone. She left a note for you. It's in your room. There's a note for you, too, Michael."

Nick barely heard her words over the roar of his blood as it rushed through his veins. "She left?" he asked through clenched teeth. "Where did she go?"

"She went to the airport. I don't really know where she intended to go from there."

His eyes narrowed. "She doesn't have a car. How did she get to the airport? And more importantly, how did she get out of that room without anyone seeing her?"

Another visible hard swallow. "There's a service entrance in the back. She used that. And she asked me to call her a cab."

"You let her go—*helped* her leave—without saying a word to anyone? Without knowing if she's even okay?" he asked, incredulous.

Her gaze shifted from him over to her brother, who was now bent over at the waist, head in hands, looking like he might puke. She rubbed a hand over Michael's back and sounded miserable as she said, "I did. It's what she said she wanted. She asked me to help her, begged me, really—"

"And I asked you to fucking stay out of it," he interrupted, seething. "To leave it alone. To let them sort it all out themselves. And you just couldn't do it, could you?"

She straightened, her expression darkening. "I didn't do anything wrong. She asked for my help, and I helped her. That's all. The decision to leave was hers."

"Leading the witness, counselor?" He threw her own words back at her with a sneer. "You're real good at getting people to do what you want, all while making them think it was their decision, aren't you?"

Grace reared back as if he'd slapped her, but her shocked expression twisted quickly into anger. "Oh, okay. I get it. Here we go. Another stupid disagreement and you're lashing out at me. Again. Getting pissed off and saying horrible things to me seems to be your go-to, Nick. Well, guess what? This wasn't my fault. I've stomped down every single instinct I had about this wedding since day *one* because of *you*, because of a promise I made to *you*. I knew this was going to go wrong, and I did nothing, for *you*. She'd already made up her mind about the wedding before I went into that room. That room that *you*—" she punctuated her sentence with a sharp poke to his chest "—*asked* me to go into. But you're conveniently forgetting all that, aren't you?"

"This isn't about me," he spit out through his clenched teeth.

Her fisted hands shot to her hips. "So are you saying I

shouldn't have helped her? Are you saying you wouldn't have helped her leave if she'd asked you?"

"Of course I would've helped her. But you should've told me what was going on."

"This isn't about you," she shot back with a sneer of her own.

"Is someone going to tell me what the fuck is going on? Where's Sadie?" Gage asked from behind them as they faced off.

Before anyone could answer, Michael straightened and clocked Gage in the jaw with a wild right hook. "You son of a bitch," Michael shouted. "If you had anything to do with her running away, I'll kill you."

"Michael!" Sarah gasped.

Ruthie shook her head, disgusted. "That was the worst punch I've ever seen. A bitch-slap would've been more effective than that. I'm disappointed in you, boy! Apparently all that hockey we used to watch was for nothing."

From his position on the floor, Gage shifted his jaw from side to side, probably trying to make sure it still worked. "I was in the bar all fucking night. How could I have had anything to do with any of this, Michael?"

"Don't tell me you're not happy about this," Michael argued. "I've seen the way you look at her."

"Of course I'm not happy," Gage grumbled, climbing to his feet. "You're family, dumbass. I wouldn't ever do anything to hurt you. But that punch was the only one you'll get for free. Try that again and I'm hitting back."

"Betcha ten that *Gage* can throw a decent right hook," Ruthie offered to no one in particular.

"I swear to God I thought I packed an extra Kindle charger," David muttered, patting his pockets down again.

"Oh, God," Sarah cried, "Did she run away with my dress?"

Grace let out a disgusted growl. "I have the dress, mom. Dad, there's an extra charger in my room. Please go get it. Ruthie, no one is hitting anyone again. Michael, Gage didn't say anything to Sadie to make her leave."

Nick's eyes narrowed on her again. "That was carefully worded, counselor," he said. "He didn't *say* anything to her, but he had something to do with why she left, didn't he?"

Grace's mouth opened, and she exchanged a loaded glance with Gage, but neither said anything.

"That's it," Michael snapped at Gage, "You're dead."

And with that, he threw another punch. But this time, Gage was ready for it. Gage caught Michael's fist, yanked his arm behind him, and slammed him face-first into the wall.

"I'm telling you," Gage hissed in Michael's ear, "I didn't do anything. Was I attracted to her? Hell, yes. But I'd never do anything about it. I told you already: you're my family, idiot. The only real family I've ever had. I wouldn't ever do anything to hurt you. You've always been more than just my cousin, okay? You're my brother."

Michael stopped struggling against Gage's hold when Gage repeated, quietly this time, "You're my brother."

Sarah pulled a wad of toilet paper out of her handbag and swiped at the tears rolling down her cheeks. "Oh, that was just lovely, Gage."

With a snort, Gage let go of Michael, who shoved off the wall and spun around to face Gage again. Everyone seemed to hold their breath while the two men faced each other down. But after a moment of intense eye contact, Michael grabbed Gage in a bear hug. As dude-like back-slapping ensued, Nick knew all was well between the cousins/brothers. He wished he could say the same for his sister.

And for him and Grace, for that matter.

"I'm glad this is all working out for you guys," Nick began, struggling not to yell at anyone, "but my sister just left her own wedding. Alone. She was fine *yesterday*, so whatever made her decide to leave happened *today*."

His eyes shifted back to Grace, whose spine immediately stiffened, making her look much taller than she actually was. "I don't know how many more times I can say this, Nick, but her mind was made up when I went into that room. It wasn't my fault. I told you I wouldn't interfere and I didn't."

Sure, not directly. But she was smart enough to manipulate Sadie and Michael—and maybe even Gage—into whatever outcome she wanted. And she'd made it clear from the beginning that she wasn't in favor of the wedding. He knew her intentions were good—she was just trying to save a couple of kids from getting married way too young—but the outcome was the same. His baby sister was devastated and alone, and he hadn't been able to do a damn thing to help her.

Grace had *robbed* him of the chance to do anything to help her.

"You believe me…don't you?" Grace asked, sounding unsure.

He didn't answer, but the look on his face must've told her exactly what she didn't want to hear, because her uncertainty vanished as she looked up at him with loathing. "Well, if that's how you feel, you should just go," she bit out.

"That's the best idea I've heard all day," he said, and left, feeling Grace's eyes on his back the whole way.

Chapter Thirty-five

The silence left in the wake of Nick's departure was deafening. Grace wasn't sure how much more of it she could take.

"That was disgraceful."

Grace tore her eyes off Nick's retreating back and glanced over at Ruthie, who'd just wheeled up beside her.

I was wrong. Silence is better than this.

Hoping Michael couldn't hear them from his place at the bar with Gage, Grace said, "There's nothing disgraceful about Sadie leaving. She did what she had to do. It wasn't Michael's fault."

Ruthie snorted. "I'm not talking about that. That girl did Michael a favor by leaving. That whole wedding would've been a dumpster fire. I'm talking about you and that Irishman."

Grace barely resisted the urge to bang her head on the wall. "Sorry if you were embarrassed by—" *the sight of my heart breaking right here in this very spot? My humiliation at having the man I love think that I planned to ruin his sister's life?* "—our disagreement."

The old woman let out what sounded like a combo snort/belch, and that's when Grace knew she'd been hitting the bar. Great. Ruthie didn't exactly get sun-shinier with a few drinks onboard. "Why don't I take you back to your room, Grandma? We can just—"

"I wasn't talking about your *disagreement*," she interrupted with an exasperated huff. "I meant you two idiots arguing about nothing. You're both just too chicken shit to tell each other how you feel, so you're wrecking everything. It's like something out of a shitty romantic comedy with that Bollocks woman."

"Pretty sure you mean Bullock. Sandra Bullock, Grandma," Grace muttered.

Ruthie waved her hand dismissively. "Whatever. You know what I mean."

"It's none of your business," came a whisper from behind them.

Grace looked over her shoulder at her mother. "What was that, Mom?"

"Yes, do speak up, Sarah," Ruthie said dryly. "I'm sure you have something *invaluable* to contribute."

For a split second, Grace thought her mother was going to slink away and keep her mouth shut. After all, the most her mother ever did to defy Ruthie was throw a couple of passive-aggressive gestures her way. But instead, Sarah straightened to her full height, stared down into Ruthie's narrowed eyes, and said, "I *said* it's none of your business what goes on between Grace and Nick. None. Of. Your. Business. Grace didn't ask for your opinion. Just like *I* never asked for your opinion all the times you gave it to me over the years."

Her voice rising with every sentence, she added, "No one ever asks for your opinion, old woman, so why don't you just shut the fuck up?"

Grace's eyes widened in shock. She'd never in her *life* heard her mother say "fuck," even when she burned her thumb on her baking sheet or stubbed her toe on the leg of the coffee table. On the other side of the room at the bar, Gage started a slow clap that all of the wait staff and the bartender quickly joined in on.

Ruthie shifted her gaze to David. "Are you going to allow your wife to speak to your mother like that, Davey?"

"Davey" walked over slowly, looking dazed like he'd just awakened from a coma, and took his place at his wife's side. That's when Grace noticed he'd set his Kindle down on the bar. It was the first time she'd seen him without it all week. "Yes, Mother, I am," he said. Then he shifted his gaze to his wife and said, "I love you."

Sarah laid both her palms on his face and kissed him square on the mouth. "Of course you do." Then she moved behind Ruthie's chair. "Now, I have flights to book and arrangements to make, so let's get you back to your room so that you can rest, Mother, um, I mean, Ruthie."

Ruthie wiped her nose with the back of her hand. "I suppose it's alright if you want to call me mother. Or not. Whatever," she grumbled.

Sarah smiled a cat-who-ate-the-canary smile, winked at her husband, and said, “I’d love to. Mother.”

As they walked away, Gage walked over and pressed a shot glass full of something that looked like tequila into Grace’s hand. “At least someone got their happily-ever-after today, huh?” he asked.

Grace laughed without humor and downed her shot. Yep, definitely tequila, she thought as it burned a path down to her stomach. “Yeah. I guess one out of five will have to do.”

“Nick’s probably just hurt that Sadie asked for your help to escape instead of his,” Gage told her. “You realize his little blow-up probably didn’t really have anything to do with you, right?”

Instead of answering, Grace grabbed *his* shot glass and downed *his* tequila. She didn’t want to talk about Nick. Not anymore. She’d been letting her heart do her thinking for the past week. It was totally irrational to even consider a future with somebody she’d just met, especially somebody who thought she was a manipulative liar. Time to start using her great big, Notre Dame-educated brain to do her thinking for her instead of delegating the job to her heart.

And her brain was telling her that *his little blow-up* today was the best thing that could’ve happened to them. It was time to go back to LA—alone—and get on with her life.

She’d just have to ignore her pathetic heart, which practically wept at the thought of never seeing Nick again.

Gage opened his mouth to say something else, but snapped it shut when a shriek split the air, the sound so shrill Grace winced and had to cover her ears.

"Jesus," Grace said when the noise died down into quiet whimpers, sobs, and nearly incoherent prayers. "What the hell is *that*?"

Gage shook his head. "No clue. Maybe someone's skinning a senator's daughter for the woman suit he's making in his basement?"

"I told you never to mention that movie to me again," Grace said with a shudder.

"It puts the lotion on or it gets the hose—"

Grace slapped her palms back over her ears. "Stop it!"

He chuckled and said something she couldn't hear—because, covered ears—but then his expression turned serious as he glanced at someone over Grace's shoulder.

She took her hands off her ears and whirled around to find Lucille standing in front of her, wearing only one high-heel shoe, a mini-skirt that looked to be on backwards, and a half-buttoned, leopard-print silk blouse.

Lucille smoothed a hand over her head—which was sporting the worst case of bedhead Grace had ever seen—and gave Gage a wide, nervous smile. "Hey, there, uh, doc," she sputtered, obviously trying to look like she hadn't just stumbled out of a natural disaster. "Can I get you to come help me for a quick sec?"

Gage immediately switched from tipsy wedding guest to doctor in less time than it took Grace to drag her eyes away from the great expanse of cleavage Lucille was flashing. "Are you alright?" he asked, already looking her over, eyes cold, assessing her for injuries.

"Oh, yeah, sure, I'm fine. It's, uh, not me who needs help."

"Wait here," he told Grace as he hurried to follow Lucille, who'd started tottering at a pretty impressive clip on her one ridiculously high heel toward the bathroom on the opposite side of the reception hall.

It'd been a shitty, shitty day. Grace was tired and heartbroken. There was no way she was missing out on whatever was going on in that bathroom. Misery loved company, right?

So into the unisex bathroom they went, Lucille, followed by Gage, with Grace right on his heels. And what they saw there made Grace completely question the whole misery-loves-company thing.

Brad lay on the bathroom floor, completely naked, but for a wad of paper towels he was holding over his groin. Tears streamed down his cheeks, and he was sucking in great gulps of air in between uttering what sounded like stuttering, broken prayers.

Gage stumbled to a stop, causing Grace to run into his back. "Jesus, Grace," he muttered, "I told you to wait out there for me."

Grace bit down on her bottom lip. "I was curious," she whispered, horrified.

Gage shoved a hand through his hair and shifted back into doctor mode. "Alright, what's going on here?"

Brad glanced at Lucille, wide-eyed and panicked. She gave him an encouraging nod and said, "Go ahead and show him, honey. It'll be OK."

Honey? Grace thought. When had *that* happened? But then Brad lifted the paper towels off his groin and Grace had to stifle a shriek at the sight that assailed her poor, unsuspecting eyes.

"Holy Mother of God," she said, barely resisting the urge to trace the sign of the cross over her chest. "What is *that*?"

Gage cocked his head to one side and after a moment said, "Huh. That's a penile fracture. You don't see one of those every day. Caused by blunt-force trauma. How did that happen?"

Brad started sobbing again, so Lucille answered for him. "Well, we were, you know, having an *intimate* moment. He was there on the counter and I was, you know, on top of him," she said, twirling a strand of hair around her index finger, "and then we heard sort of a *popping* sound. I got off him, and that's when he rolled off the counter onto the floor."

Gage winced. Brad sobbed louder.

"Misalignment, huh?" Gage asked. "Came down on him wrong?"

Lucille straightened and raised a brow at him. "I can assure you I came down on him just *right*. But, yes, he slipped out and might've, uh, gotten *bent* under me at an odd angle."

"I promise I'll never be curious again," Grace muttered fervently.

"Can you fix him, doc?" Lucille asked.

Gage shook his head. "No. That's a surgical fix, and I don't have privileges at any hospitals around here. Grace, can you call 911, please? We'll need an ambulance."

"Couldn't we just drive him to the hospital?" Grace asked.

"We could," Gage answered, "but I don't want to."

Well, it was kind of hard to argue with that logic.

Half an hour later, Brad was loaded into an ambulance and on his way to a local hospital. Lucille stayed at his side the whole time. Her devotion would have been touching…if she hadn't broken his penis and all.

Gage threw an arm around Grace's shoulders as they made their way back through the hotel's lobby. "Well, that was fun."

She snorted. "If by 'fun' you mean terrifying and possibly

permanently scarring. Then, sure, it was *fun*."

"Hey, we had a fucking horrific day. The woman who is maybe, possibly…*something* to me ran away without a word, my cousin punched me in the face, and the only flight home I could get us isn't until tomorrow and it has a three-hour layover in Detroit. And your whole thing with Nick was a shit-show of epic proportions. That penile fracture was a gift from Karma herself. We *deserved* that penile fracture. We *earned* that penile fracture today, Grace."

"He's going to be alright, isn't he?" Grace asked, biting her lip. "I won't feel right laughing at him unless I know he's going to be alright. Because *that* would be bad karma for me."

"He'll be fine. It's a relatively easy fix with typically good surgical outcomes."

Oh, well, in that case…

Grace's quiet chuckles mixed with Gage's deeper ones. Before long, Grace was giggling and gasping for breath while leaning on Gage for support.

She knew she only giggled like this in times of high stress. It was the kind of giggling that kept her from crying. But it wouldn't work forever. It was like trying to plug a hole in a dam with a piece of wadded-up chewing gum.

Eventually the dam would break and the flood would come.

Gage must have known what was about to happen because his laughter stalled out completely. Without a word, he tugged her into his arms and wrapped her up in a tight hug. Unfortunately, that little bit of kindness and understanding was all it took to break her.

"It'll be okay," he told her over and over again as her laughter melted into sobs.

Chapter Thirty-six

Nick read Sadie's letter seventeen times. Seventeen times. It wasn't that the letter was so complicated it required seventeen reads. But every now and then, as Nick was learning, it took a while for the human brain to comprehend even the simplest of messages.

Especially when the messages told him he'd been a complete dumbass who now owed the mother of all apologies to the woman he loved.

Grace had been telling the truth. She didn't have anything to do with Sadie calling off the wedding and running away. Sadie had acted like the stupid kid she was all on her own. Even if Grace hadn't called her a cab and helped her escape without being seen, someone else would have. And Nick now knew he wouldn't have been able to talk Sadie off the ledge. The wedding had been doomed and nothing he could've said would've fixed anything.

Hearing you explain how you know who "the one" is was a wake-up call for me, Nicky. I thought all I ever wanted was a family, but now I want what you and Grace have. Michael is wonderful and perfect and I love him, but he's not the one. He deserves someone better than me. And deep down, I know I deserve better, too, but I'm just too messed up to go after it right now. I have to find myself before I can find the one who is meant for me.

So, technically, he supposed, if anyone could be blamed for Sadie's epic case of cold feet, it was Nick, which just made everything worse. Especially since instead of telling Grace he loved her, he'd accused her of purposefully sabotaging his sister's life and marriage.

If he could kick his own ass, he would. He was going to have to do some pretty epic groveling to get Grace to forgive him this time. Pretty words and flowers and orgasms weren't going to cut it. At this point, he wasn't even sure jewelry, the top tier of I'm-sorry-I-was-a-dumbass gifts, would fix what he'd fucked up. Maybe he could—

A tentative knock on the door separating his room from Grace's snapped him out of his mental calculations.

He was at the door and yanked it open so fast Grace's hand was still poised to knock when they came face to face. Her eyes were red-rimmed and puffy, which made him want to kick his own ass even more than he had before. And that was saying a lot, because he was *really* pissed off at himself.

Nick expelled a huge breath before blurting, "God, Grace, I was such a fucking idiot. I have no idea what I was even thinking. I know you didn't have anything to do with why Sadie left. I'm so, so sorry."

Her eyes narrowed. "How do you know I didn't have anything to do with why Sadie left? Is it because you realized I would never do anything to intentionally hurt Sadie and Michael—or because Sadie told you so in her letter?"

He had a feeling she didn't want to hear him say *both*, even though it was true. But judging by the look on her face, he wasn't even sure there *was* a right answer to her question. Honesty would have to do, he supposed. "I *would've* known that, had I not been so scared for Sadie, and pissed off that I'd failed at trying to take care of her again. I *do* know that you'd never do anything like that. It just…took me a little while to clear my head and see that."

Grace stared at him so hard for a moment that he wondered if she was trying to bore a hole through his skull with nothing but the power of her eyes. But eventually, she nodded and said, "It's okay. I understand, and I forgive you."

If he hadn't been so fucking relieved to hear those words, he might've noticed how flat her voice sounded, or how cold her eyes looked. There was nothing at all Grace-like in how she looked or sounded in that moment. But relief overruled his common sense and he let out all his pent-up tension in the form of a huge sigh as he reached for her. "Grace, you won't regret it. In fact, I need to tell you what I was *trying* to tell you earlier, before everything happened. The truth is that I lov—"

Grace held up a hand to interrupt him and took a huge step back, out of his reach.

All the relief Nick had felt only a moment ago died a hard, swift death. Suddenly the space between them felt like the fucking Continental Divide. Nick's entire body went cold. "What's wrong?" he asked, not at all sure he really wanted her answer.

"Look," she began, her eyes lifting, but not meeting his, "today was a really good reminder of what we are. This whole thing has just happened so fast. If we keep this up, if you move to LA, we're really no better than Sadie and Michael. We just don't know each other well enough for that."

He wanted to keep a cool head this time, to not go off the deep end and say things he shouldn't. That's what had got him in the mess, after all. But he couldn't stop himself from saying, "That's such bullshit. We're not anything like Sadie and Michael. We're grown-ups, first of all. You're not at all confused about who you are, and neither am I. And I *know* you, Grace. We might not have known each other for a long time, but I *know* you."

That brought a little heat to her eyes. Just not the good kind, sadly. "No, you don't," she said. "If you *did* know me, you would've known that I didn't intentionally ruin Sadie and Michael's wedding."

His chin hit his chest. "So you don't really forgive me. That's okay. I understand. We can fix this. I just—"

"No. I *do* forgive you. I need to thank you, actually."

Never had the words *thank you* sounded so terrifying. "Why would you thank me?"

She shrugged her shoulders in a careless gesture that was at odds with her tight expression. "We've been caught up in all the…physical stuff. The chemistry between us. We haven't been using our heads. Today you reminded me that I need to be logical, rational about our relationship."

Which was the most ridiculous thing he'd ever heard. There was nothing logical or rational about emotions and relationships. They were messy and complicated and irrational. Truly rational people would *never* let themselves fall in love. "And what would a logical, rational person do about our relationship?"

A little furrow appeared between her brows. "A logical, rational person would stick to our original agreement. I said I'd be with you for one week. Our one week is up. It's time to go back to our real lives now."

Nick grabbed her shoulders firmly enough to keep her from moving further away from him—because *fuck* the Continental Divide—but gently enough not to hurt or scare her. "My real life *is* you, Grace. I love you. I don't give a fuck if we've only known each other a week, and I don't give a fuck about *logical* and *rational*. I love you."

She shut her eyes and wrapped her arms around her stomach as if his words had hurt her. "I don't want to hear that. This is all too much, Nick. The thing with Sadie and Michael, you living on the other end of the country, the fact that we've had two terrible, ugly fights in the course of only a few days…I just can't do it. You said yourself when this thing started that you didn't *do* complicated. Well, we *complicate* each other, Nick." She shook her head sadly. "I'm going home. By myself."

Well, this is not at all how he expected his first-ever *I love you* declaration to play out. "Grace, I don't think it's all as complicated as we've made it seem. The thing with Sadie and Michael is over. It doesn't have anything to do with us. I already told you I'm more than happy to move to be closer to you. There's nothing tying me to Chicago anymore. I won't rush you into anything more. After I move, we'll date like normal people. And as for our fights…well, those were my fault. I've never done this before. I'll surely fuck things up every now and then. But if you're willing to try, I *know* we can make it work."

Her head came up and she finally looked him right in the eye, and he knew before she said it that they were over. She was done with him. He'd finally managed to screw things up with her irreparably.

"I'm not willing to try," she said, her voice sounding horrible and firm and nothing at all like her normal voice. "We're just…too different."

Because you're poor, dumb trailer trash and she's a lawyer. She's too good for you.

Nick forced himself to shake the negative thoughts off. Fuck those old insecurities! Shit like that wasn't going to help his cause. It never had.

He couldn't stop himself from yanking her into his arms. "Don't do this," he whispered. "If you need some space, I'll give it to you. But don't make it forever."

He kissed her, hard and desperate. For a second, he thought she was going to kiss him back, but she didn't. So he just pressed his cheek against hers and held on for dear life.

Her breathing hitched, and as a single, lonely tear rolled down her cheek, he thought—*hoped*—he had her. He thought she was going to change her mind and give him the second—or third—chance he didn't really deserve but wanted more than his next breath.

But his hope was ground to dust under her stiletto as she pushed shakily out of his arms, leaned up to kiss his cheek, and said, "Goodbye, Nick."

Nick rubbed his chest absently as he watched her walk away, wondering if *this* was what Michael was feeling right now. Because if it was, he owed the kid a giant apology for every nasty thing he'd thought and said about him over the course of the week. *No one* deserved to feel like this.

Chapter Thirty-seven

Since all her girlfriends were in LA and not answering their damn phones, poor Gage got stuck with the responsibility of plying Grace with alcohol and ice cream to get her over her breakup.

After two hours or so of listening to her sob and moan, he decided her ice cream intake was slowing down her alcohol intake. She needed the ice cream, but she *really* needed the alcohol. So, in all his infinite wisdom, Gage suggested mixing the vodka directly into her tub of Cherry Garcia. And thus, the Smirnoff Smoothie was born.

Sadly, the genius of the idea just made her sob harder, because the first person she'd wanted to call and talk to about the Smirnoff Smoothie was Nick.

Nick *totally* would've appreciated the genius of the Smirnoff Smoothie.

But the next day, as Grace eyed the hollowed-out tub of ice cream and four empty bottles of vodka—she was pretty sure Gage had contributed mightily to the downfall of the vodka, but sadly, the ice cream was all her—she started doubting the Smirnoff Smoothie as a viable breakup cure-all.

"You look something a cat puked up," Gage told her as he started an IV in her arm to replenish her fluids.

Grace lifted her head and squinted at him out of one eye—

she'd learned pretty quickly that opening both eyes fully felt like someone was jamming a cattle prod into her eye socket—while she contemplated giving him the finger. Ultimately deciding that would require too much effort, she instead asked him, "Why don't you look like death on a stick? You drank every bit as much as I did. And where the hell did you even get an IV?"

"I drank more than you did. I started drinking a full day before you and never really stopped. But I also weigh more and ate more real food than you did last night—ice cream doesn't count. And I've always held my liquor better than you. The IV came from the medical supply store down the street. I picked it up after our last vodka run. I figured you'd be needing it."

She wanted to argue about him holding his liquor better than her, but kept her mouth shut. After all, he was right, and there was that whole *effort* thing to consider. Using up what little energy she had at the moment seemed like a bad idea. "Do you think this will work?" she asked, gesturing with her chin to the IV.

He shrugged as he hung the IV bag on the pole. "Restorative IVs aren't magical cure-alls. The only real hangover cure is time. But this'll probably take the edge off and make it so you can catch your flight home this afternoon without puking on the plane."

Thoughts of puking on the plane just brought up memories of the last time she'd puked on a plane, which brought up memories of Nick, which just made her sad and contemplating Smirnoff

Smoothies again. She needed a subject change, and fast. “Did you check on Michael last night?”

Gage sat down next to her on the couch. “He’s fine. He was with your mom and she was trying to set him up with some blonde when I saw them.”

Grace rolled her eyes. “I suppose she’s thinking he can just screw someone else until he doesn’t miss Sadie anymore?”

Gage raised a brow at her. “I guess he could just drink Smirnoff Smoothies until he needs a restorative IV instead.”

She sniffed. “Touché.”

“Everyone copes with a breakup and loss differently. Don’t be judge-y.”

Grace leaned her head back against the sofa. “And how will you deal with your loss in this whole thing?”

“I didn’t lose anything,” he said, his voice flatter than day-old Diet Coke. “I felt…something for a girl who apparently didn’t feel anything back, because she left without a word.” He shrugged. “No loss. I move on.”

“And hook up with blondes?” she asked gently.

He glanced over at her and smirked. “If they’re lucky.”

Grace reached over and patted his knee, careful not to disturb her IV. "They *would* be lucky. Sadie would've been lucky to have you. And just for the record, she *did* feel something back. She just didn't know what to do with that feeling. Or *any* feelings, apparently."

"Fuckin' kids these days," he muttered in his best old-man get-off-my-lawn voice. "Don't know nothin'."

"Yeah, you laugh so you won't have to feel."

"Yeah, well, you drink so *you* won't have to feel."

Another sniff. "Touché."

"You know," he began conversationally, "you're a dumbass if you don't go after him."

She narrowed her eyes on him, incredulous. "I'm a dumbass for not going after someone who believed I was capable of horrible things? *Twice*?"

He rolled his eyes at her. "He didn't *really* think that. He got angry in the heat of the moment. *Twice*. No big deal. He got over it, and he apologized. He's passionate. Passionate people yell. It's when they *don't* yell anymore that you have a problem."

Grace immediately thought of Brad. They'd never yelled at each other. They hadn't had one single fight, until the day he admitted to cheating on her. They got along perfectly, right up until they didn't. Was that because they were well-suited, or because they were apathetic?

The buzzing of her phone disrupted her thoughts, and her hopes rose, thinking maybe it was Nick on the other line. She lunged to answer the call before she remembered she'd told Nick goodbye, and the chances of him calling her this morning were slim to nil.

Her hopes were completely crushed when she read *doucheBrad calling* on the screen. Ugh. Could her day get any worse?

Grace answered the call reluctantly and grumbled the world's most half-hearted greeting.

"Oh, Grace, thank God I caught you. And thank you so much for answering," Brad babbled, sounding extremely happy for a man with a broken penis.

"How are you doing, Brad?" she asked, even though she found it hard to care. Asking seemed like the polite thing to do, though.

"I'm fantastic. The surgery was a success. The doctors are confident that I'll, um, gain back full function."

Even though she was in an exceedingly bad mood and hadn't ever really benefited much from Brad's *full function* while they were married, Grace bit back an uncharitable reply. She was finding she just didn't want to hang onto her hatred of Brad anymore. "That's good, Brad," she said. "I'm happy for you."

"That's what I wanted to tell *you*, actually."

"That you're happy my penis isn't broken anymore?" she asked, thoroughly confused.

He chuckled. "No. That I'm *happy* for you. I'm glad you found someone who can make you happy."

He meant Nick. And wasn't that just a stab in the old heart? Then it occurred to her that Brad and Nick had been nothing but horrible to each other all week. "I thought you hated Nick."

"Oh, I did, trust me. And he's still not who I would've pictured you ending up with. But, you know how you always hear about people who've had near-death experiences coming back from the brink with such *clarity*? Well, that's what happened to me, Grace."

You broke your penis during rough bathroom sex with a random woman you picked up in a casino, dumbass. You were never near death. But saying that was beyond pointless, so Grace kept her mouth shut yet again.

"When I woke up after surgery," he went on, "everything was so clear, clearer than it had ever been. You, me, our marriage…everything suddenly made *sense* to me. I thought about what I overheard Nick saying about you the night before the wedding. Well, I didn't really *overhear* as much I was spying on him and shamelessly eavesdropping, if I'm being honest. But regardless, it was his words that made me realize that no matter how much I'd always loved you—and how much I still do love you—you're just not *the one* for me. More importantly, I'm not *the one* for you."

Wait…what? "What exactly did you hear Nick saying about me, Brad?"

"Oh, well, nothing that he probably hasn't said to you a hundred times, but he said quite a lot, really. What really stuck with me, though, was when he said you were his balance. The sunlight to his darkness. He's quite poetic, isn't he?"

Tears filled Grace's eyes and she suddenly felt like a fist had closed around her windpipe. "He said that?" she choked out.

"Indeed," Brad answered. "Which is what made me realize that the better man had won in this instance. I just had to tell you that I won't be troubling you to reconcile anymore. I'll leave you to your happily-ever-after, and I'll be off trying to find my own."

It was the most civilized, adult conversation she'd had with Brad since the divorce, and Grace did the whole thing in a daze. Brad's words—or rather, *Nick's* words—rattled around in her brain the whole time.

When she ended the call, she turned to Gage, who appeared to be playing some kind of zombie-killing game on his phone. "He really did love me," she said miserably.

"I would hope so," Gage answered, not looking up from his screen. "He married you and all. He's an ass, but he's not stupid or unfeeling."

"I was talking about Nick. He really did love me."

Gage snorted. "Duh. Anyone could see that." He hit pause on his game. "Wait…did you break things off with him because you thought he didn't love you?"

Her reasons for breaking things off with Nick suddenly seemed kind of fuzzy. "I broke things off with him because it's all so…complicated. He lives on the other side of the country, he was about to be my brother-in-law, we haven't really known each other that long…and, yeah, I guess I didn't think he really could love me after such a short time of knowing me. I figured he'd realize he'd made a big mistake if he followed me out to LA, then he'd leave and I'd be crushed."

"And how do you feel about him?" Gage asked, sounding exasperated.

"I love him," she answered without hesitation.

He leaned forward, resting his elbows on his splayed knees and giving her a hard side-eye. "So, let me get this straight. The dude loves you. You love him. And you dumped him on the off chance that he *might* one day decide shit is moving too fast and dump *you*?"

Well, it sounded really teenager-y when he put it like that. "Well, yes."

Gage stood up and let out a disgusted sigh. "You dumbass. If I'd known that, I never would've made you Smirnoff Smoothies."

Grace frowned up at him. "Why'd you *think* I dumped him?"

He threw his hands up in frustration. "I thought he loved you more than you loved him, and you wanted to let him down gently but felt really bad about it. Jesus, if I'd known you were just too chicken-shit to take a chance on him, I would've dumped you off with your mom."

"That's so mean," she whispered.

Gage jabbed his index finger in her direction. "If you don't run him down and beg his forgiveness, you don't deserve him. And if you can't make it work with a guy who loves you as much as Nick clearly loves you, you should just go the fuck home and buy a dozen cats and take up knitting, because you're gonna die a bitter, lonely old woman."

His words were the equivalent of a slap to the face. A reality bitch-slap. It occurred to her then that she'd never really given Nick a fair chance. In the back of her mind, she'd always assumed he'd leave her, just like Brad did. She'd lawyered him. She'd collected the little mistakes he'd made and kept them as evidence in her case against him. Had used them as an excuse to end things with him before he could hurt her.

"Oh my God," she muttered. "I'm a dumbass!"

Gage nodded. "This is what I'm saying."

As fast as her fingers would go, she punched Nick's number into her phone. The call went right to voice mail. She leapt off the couch like it was on fire. "I have to find him! I need to talk to him now."

"That could be a problem."

She fought back a growl of pure frustration. "There's no problem. I know what I need to do. I have to make this work."

The look he shot her bordered on pity. "It's a problem because Nick left an hour ago."

Fuuuuccccckkkkk.

Chapter Thirty-eight

All those romantic comedies that showed the beautiful, put-together heroine racing to the airport—wind-whipped, perfect hair flying behind her—to declare her undying love to the hero, and the two of them embracing dramatically in front of the gate before his plane departed were full of shit. Absolute shit.

The truth of a last-minute airport run was much less screen-worthy. First of all, finding out where Nick was had practically taken an act of God. As it turned out, the airlines and the Department of Homeland Security weren't terribly inclined to give out the flight info of their air marshals. Grace assumed she was now on more than a few terrorist watch- lists thanks to all the inquiries she'd made.

In the end, it had only been with the help of the smarmy air marshal she'd met at the airport when she'd been detained that she'd been able to get Nick's travel itinerary. She wasn't sure if she should be thankful, or creeped-out that he remembered who she was ("the blonde with the rack") after their one brief meeting. She supposed she should just be grateful he thought Nick needed to get laid enough to break all his employer's rules and risk losing his job.

And as she raced from one end of the airport to the other, uncombed hair sticking to her sweaty forehead, missing one shoe (God only knew where she'd lost *that*), wearing Gage's T-shirt (she'd puked Smirnoff Smoothie all over hers, apparently) and a pair of flannel pajama pants that said "sassy" across her ass, Grace imagined she was about as far removed from a romantic comedy heroine as a body could get. Not to mention the ginormous hit her bank account had taken when she had to book the last- minute, first-class ticket that would allow her a seat on Nick's flight.

But none of that mattered, because she was *here*. It looked like everyone else had boarded, but she'd *made* it. She'd finally get a chance to tell Nick how she felt and beg for his forgiveness.

Gasping for breath, she bent over at the waist and handed her ticket to the pretty brunette gate attendant, who gave her a serious-looking side-eye. "Ma'am, are you alright?"

"Fine…" *gasp* "…stupid running…" *gasp* "…out of shape…" *gasp* "…Smirnoff Smoothies…" *gasp* "air marshal…" *gasp* "this plane…" "…love him" *gasp* "need to tell him…" *gasp* "…now."

Her eyes widened. "Oh my God, did you do the romantic-comedy-last-minute-airport-run for Marshal McHottie?" She jumped up and down and clapped her hands together like a kid. "That's so awesome!" Then she stopped, "Wait, are you the reason he's so grumpy this morning?"

Grace grimaced. "Ugh. Probably."

She raised a brow at her. "Girl, you've got your work cut out for you. But let's get you on that plane, okay? And if it all works out, I'm going to expect an invite to your wedding. And if it *doesn't* work out, you're going to give me his phone number, because I've been trying to get it for three years, and that is just too much man to go to waste, am I right?"

Since Grace pretty much would've promised the other woman a kidney at that point to get on the plane, she readily agreed and quickly found herself tucked into her ridiculously overpriced first-class seat, waiting for takeoff, after which she'd be allowed to move back into business class, where Nick was seated.

Leaning her head back against her seat and squeezing her eyes shut, Grace did what she did every time she got on a plane.

She prayed.

Only this time, the prayer she sent heavenward didn't have anything to do with her request not to plummet from the sky in a fireball of death.

Please, God, don't let me screw this up. That ticket-taker was super-cute, and I really don't want to have to give her Nick's phone number if this whole thing doesn't go my way.

Nick had already been tired and pissed-off at the world when his boss called and asked him to pick up a flight to Boston, filling in for a fellow marshal who'd gotten the flu. But now, as he sat in his aisle seat next to a burly, hairy dude who smelled like broiled beef and a little old lady who wouldn't stop showing him pictures of her seven or eight *hundred* grandkids, Nick started seriously questioning the life choices that had gotten him to this place in his life.

This was a whole new level of pissed off for him. He was tired of this plane and everyone on it, and the flight couldn't be over fast enough for his peace of mind.

It didn't help that his mind and his heart were firmly back in Indianapolis—maybe on their way back to LA by now—with Grace.

Damn it, he hadn't wanted to leave without saying anything to her, but Gage said she was passed out—literally. She'd had a rough night and needed her sleep, he'd said. Since it was his fault she'd had that rough night, Nick couldn't bring himself to selfishly wake her up and beg for her forgiveness again. That wouldn't make *her* feel any better. As much as he hated it, he'd resigned himself to the fact that she might just need some time away from him to get her feelings sorted out.

And if when everything was sorted, she still didn't want anything to do with him…well, he'd blow up that bridge when he came to it. Pathetic groveling would ensue, of that he was pretty damn sure.

"And this one is of my granddaughter, Amelia," the old lady to his right said as she shoved her phone under his nose once more. "The picture doesn't really do her justice. She's pretty enough to be a model, you know. Kind of like this young lady right here…only my Amelia would never go out in public in her pajamas."

Nick lifted his eyes from the phone to see who the old lady was referring to, and almost swallowed his tongue.

Grace stood in the aisle in front of him. Her limp hair was plastered to her shiny forehead. She was wearing mismatched socks and only one house slipper, along with a man's T-shirt and ill-fitting flannel pants with little purple pineapples printed all over them. There was a pillow crease down the entire left side of her face.

He'd never seen anything more beautiful—or welcome—in his life.

He opened his mouth to speak, but she held up her hands to silence him. "Look," she said, "I need to get this out, so please don't say anything until I'm done, OK?"

That was fine, because he had no idea what he'd been about to say to her, anyway. Probably something stupid that involved begging. So he just gave her what he hoped was an encouraging nod.

She took a deep breath before blurting, "I was a complete dumbass. I *am* a complete dumbass. I was so worried about how things could go *wrong* between us that I got distracted from how perfect things actually *are* between us. You were right. The two measly little fights we had this week weren't anything that any other couple wouldn't have gone through. But the truth is that I was so scared—of you, of us, of falling in love—that I pushed you away. I used those stupid fights to push you away because somewhere in the back of my mind, I just assumed you were going to eventually leave me, and I thought that if I pushed you away first, it'd hurt less in the long run."

Tears filled her eyes, and it was all he could do not to pull her into his arms and tell her everything was going to be okay. But she must have sensed his intentions, because she raised her hands again to ward him off and squeezed her eyes shut.

"But I was wrong. I was wrong to push you away," she said, speaking much faster than before. "I couldn't stand to let you go home without telling you how I really feel. I can't let you walk away without fighting for you. You deserve someone who will fight for you, and I've done such a terrible job of that so far. After how I treated you yesterday, if you decide you don't want me anymore, I'll totally understand. But I need to tell you the truth—what I wanted to tell you the night before the wedding, but was too scared to do it. I got all caught up in thinking I needed to hear you say it first, but that's all just such bullshit. I realize that now. I didn't realize it until Gage told me you'd gone, but I realize it now."

God, she was killing him. "Grace—"

"The fact is that we *are* complicated together, Nick. The history between Sadie and Michael, the distance between us, the fact that we're so different…it makes us complicated. But I'm not afraid of that anymore. I *like* that we're so different; it keeps us interesting. I *want* you to complicate me, and I want to complicate you."

He sucked in a deep breath and held it as she impatiently

brushed her tears away with the back of her hand.

"Iloveyou," she blurted, all in one breath. "Oh, God, I love you so much I can't stand it. And I know that logically it's too soon for us to feel this way, and that we should take it slow—"

"Grace—"

"—but the thought of taking it slow and spending even another *minute* without you makes me a little nauseous, you know? And I'm not sure—"

"Grace—"

"—what else to say, except to reiterate that I—"

He grabbed her hand. "Grace!"

Her tear-filled eyes shifted from his hand on hers, up to his face. She looked terrified. "Yes?" she whispered.

"I need you to shut up," he said.

The old lady next to him sucked in a harsh breath, and the burly guy shot him a dirty look. He ignored them both as Grace nodded and said, "Okay. Sorry. I'll just—"

He squeezed her hand. "You had me at *dumbass*."

She blinked at him several times before asking, "I did?"

Nick stood up and yanked her into his arms. "You did. I came to your room to tell you I'd been called into work this morning, but you were passed out."

"You didn't leave to get away from me?"

He shook his head. "I didn't leave to get away from you. I'm never leaving you again. I love you, too, Grace."

She let out a watery chuckle. "You do?"

In answer, he kissed her with everything he had, falling in love with her all over again when she responded just as passionately. They didn't come up for air until the passengers around them started clapping and cheering. The stewardesses and the old lady next to him wiped away happy tears while the burly guy fist-bumped Grace and congratulated her on getting her man.

"I can't believe how much I love you," he whispered in her ear.

Without warning, she pulled back so fast he almost lost his grip on her. "Oh, my God!" she cried. "I'm on a plane! I got on a plane without Valium or alcohol!"

"That's good," he murmured, snagging her bottom lip between his teeth and giving it a little nip before releasing it. "When you get unruly, I'll cuff you this time. We can have more fun with that if you're sober."

She smacked his shoulder playfully and looked up at him, heart in her eyes. "No, I think you cured my fear of flying."

He kissed her again, putting his whole heart into it. When he pulled back, he couldn't help but ask, "How did you figure out where I was and make it onto this plane?"

"Well," she hedged, drawing the word out for several extra syllables, "it's complicated."

He grinned at her. "Anything worth having is, angel. Anything worth having is."

The End

Stay tuned for Gage and Sadie's story! And keep reading for a sample (a whole first chapter, really) of *Semi-Charmed*, all my stalker links, and a personal letter to my readers!

Other books by Isabel Jordan:

The Harper Hall Investigations series reading order (all books now available everywhere books are sold):

Semi-Charmed

Semi-Human

Semi-Twisted

Semi-Broken

Semi-Sane

The Harper Hall Investigations complete series boxset

A personal note from Isabel:

If you enjoyed this book, first of all, thanks! It would mean a lot to me if you would take a moment and show your support of indie authors (like me) by leaving a review. Your reviews are a very important part of helping readers discover new books.

Want to know more about me, or when the next book release is? You can email me directly at: isabel.jordan@izzyjo.com. Also feel free to stalk me on:

Bookbub: https://www.bookbub.com/authors/isabel-jordan

Facebook: https://www.facebook.com/SemiCharmedAuthor

Private readers' group (Bitch, write faster): https://www.facebook.com/groups/846416382191567/

Twitter:@izzyjord

Pinterest: https://www.pinterest.com/ijordan0345/

Website: http://www.izzyjo.com/

Sign up for updates on all things Isabel Jordan at: http://www.izzyjo.com/sign-up.html

Thanks so much, and happy reading!

About the author

The normal:

Isabel Jordan writes because it's the only profession that allows her to express her natural sarcasm and not be fired. She is a paranormal and contemporary romance author. Isabel lives in the U.S. with her husband, 11-year-old son, a neurotic shepherd mix, and a ginormous Great Dane mix named Jerkface (but don't feel bad for him. He's earned the name).

The weird:

Now that the normal stuff is out of the way, here's some weird-but-true facts that would never come up in polite conversation. Isabel Jordan:

1. Is terrified of butterflies (don't judge ... it's a real phobia called lepidopterophobia)

2. Is a lover of all things ironic (hence the butterfly on the cover of *Semi-Charmed*)

3. Is obsessed with *Supernatural*, *Game of Thrones*, *The Walking Dead*, *The* 100, *Once Upon a Time*, and *Dog Whisperer*.

4. Hates coffee. Drinks a Diet Mountain Dew every morning.

5. Will argue to the death that *Pretty in Pink* ended all wrong. (Seriously, she ends up with the guy who was embarrassed to be seen with her and not the nice guy who loved her all along? That would never fly in the world of romance novels.)

6. Would eat Mexican food every day if given the choice.

7. Reads two books a week in varied genres.

8. Refers to her Kindle as "the precious."

9. Thinks puppy breath is one of the best smells in the world.

10. Is a social media idgit. (Her husband had to explain to her what the point of Twitter was. She's still a little fuzzy on what Instagram and Pinterest do.)

11. Kicks ass at Six Degrees of Kevin Bacon.

12. Stole her tagline idea ("weird and proud") from her son. Her tagline idea was, "Never wrong, not quite right." She liked her son's idea better.

13. Breaks one vacuum cleaner a year because she ignores standard maintenance procedures (Really, you're supposed to empty the canister every time you vacuum? Does that seem excessive to anyone else?)

14. Is still mad at the WB network for cancelling *Angel* in 2004.

15. Can't find her way from her bed to her bathroom without her glasses, but refused eye surgery, even when someone else offered to pay. (They lost her at "eye flap". Seriously, look it up. Scary stuff.)

Keep reading for a sample of *Semi-Charmed*, book 1 in the Harper Hall Investigations series!

Semi-Charmed

Chapter One

Whispering Hope, New York, today

Harper Hall swatted the fast-fingered hand of yet another horny, middle-aged CPA off her ass, but resisted the urge to dump tequila in this one's lap. After all, the Prince Valiant haircut and underbite he was saddled with were punishments enough for his crimes.

"Hey, baby," Valiant's friend said as he fondled his shot glass suggestively. "Is that a mirror in your pocket? 'Cause I can definitely see myself in your pants."

Harper rolled her eyes and shot back, "Darlin', I'm not your type. I'm not inflatable."

And with that, she turned on the heel of one of her requisite six-inch platforms and started for the bar as the CPAs chortled and bumped knuckles. They were probably looking at her butt too, but Harper chose not to dwell on that, or on the fact that most of said butt was probably hanging out of her Daisy Dukes. Not her best look, to be sure.

Lanie Cale, one of the other waitresses, grabbed her arm and leaned in, shouting over the music, "Hey, can you take over for me with the guy at table five? Carlos is letting me dance tonight. I go on in ten."

Harper gave her a quick once over. Lanie was five years her junior, ten pounds lighter, and had her beat by a full cup size. If she was Lanie, she'd probably aspire to be a stripper too. But as it stood, she was stuck waiting tables with the other B-cups.

"Sure," she answered. "But, Lanie, this guy at table five…he's not a CPA, is he? I don't think I have the strength for another CPA."

"No way is this guy a CPA. I'd bet Hugh Jackman's abs on it," she promised solemnly as she disappeared into the crowd.

At that moment, the sweaty throng of dancers and customers and waitresses parted, giving Harper her first glimpse of the guy at table five.

Wow. Hugh Jackman's abs were in no danger tonight.

The guy at table five was definitely not an accountant. Serial killer, maybe. CPA…um, no.

Table five was wedged in the corner, to the extreme right of the stage, which was why no one usually wanted to sit there. But instinct told Harper this guy had refused to sit anywhere else. This was one of those never-let-anyone-sneak-up-behind-you types, maybe with a military or law enforcement background. Paranoid and probably with good reason.

Everything about him screamed tall, dark, and brooding. From the black hair long overdue for a trim to the black-on-black wardrobe, complete with biker boots and a Highlander-like leather trench, this guy was either a true rebel without a cause, or the best imitation of one she'd ever seen.

And he was drunk off his ass. Not the kind of happy, silly drunk the CPAs at table ten had going. No, Harper could tell by the way he was ignoring the half-naked dancer on stage that he was drowning his sorrows.

Ignoring Misty Mountains wasn't easy, either. Her brand new double D's were mesmerizing, and the nipples kind of followed you wherever you went like the eyes on the creepy Jesus picture in her mom's living room.

As Harper watched, he polished off a bottle of Glenlivet and set it beside two other empties. She sighed. He'd probably pass out before he remembered to tip her. God damn drunks would be the death of her.

Harper squared her shoulders and walked up to the table, then knelt beside him so he could hear her over the bassline of Bon Jovi's Lay Your Hands On Me.

"Can I get you anything else, sir? Like coffee?" Hint, hint.

He didn't even glance at her as he slid the empty bottles to the edge of the table and said, "Another bottle."

His voice sent a shiver down her spine. It was gravelly, raspy, almost like he'd growled the words instead of speaking them. Sexy.

But sexy voice or not, she wasn't about to serve him another bottle. He was probably a few inches over six feet and maybe a little over two-hundred pounds, but no one—not even a manly man like this one—could down four bottles of eighteen-year-old Glenlivet and blow a Breathalyzer that wouldn't get him immediately arrested.

"I think you've probably had enough for tonight."

He slowly glanced over at her as if he hadn't really noticed her presence until just then. When her eyes locked with his, she completely forgot what they'd been talking about. Hell, who was she kidding? She forgot how to breathe.

This had to be the most gorgeous potential serial killer she'd ever seen.

He had a dark olive complexion most women would kill for, cheekbones sharp enough to cut glass, and eyes that were either black or the deepest blue she'd ever seen—it was too dark in the club to tell for sure.

His perfectly arched black brows—and they had to be naturally perfect, because she was pretty sure this guy wouldn't be caught dead waxing—raised sardonically as his gaze moved over her.

Harper fought the urge to suck in her stomach and desperately wished her uniform was a size eight instead of a four. She had dignity in a size eight. Class, even. In a four…not so much.

He lowered his gaze to her chest, and then slowly lifted it

back to her eyes. "I doubt they're paying you to think, sunshine." Sliding the empty bottles even closer to her, he repeated, "Another bottle."

He'd said it very slowly, deliberately, in a manner most people reserved for slow-witted children and foreigners. The only part of her that wasn't at all impressed with the guy's fallen-angel face—which just happened to be her Sicilian temper—kicked in at that point.

Harper straightened and snagged the bottles off the table, preparing to verbally flay him, but just when she'd figured out exactly how many four-letter words she could hurl at him in one sentence, a premonition hit her hard.

People often asked her what premonitions felt like. Imagine someone punching a hole through your forehead and making a fist around your brain, she always told them. This premonition was no different.

Harper staggered forward and planted one palm on the table to steady herself as images assailed her: a young, blonde woman in an alley pinned to a dumpster by a man twice her size.

A vampire, she knew instinctively. Cold chills always shot down her spine when she saw them.

Harper sucked in a deep breath and forced herself to concentrate on details other than the victim, just like Sentry taught her so many years ago. Instead, she tried to picture the dumpster, the buildings around it, street signs…anything that might tell her where this girl was so she could call the police and get her some help.

And then she saw a logo printed on the side of the dumpster as big as life. Kitty Kat Palace.

Holy shit, the vamp and his victim were here.

Harper staggered back toward the kitchen, shoving drunks and other waitresses out of her way. In the kitchen, she tipped a wooden stool on its side and stomped on one of the legs.

She bent down and scooped it up, testing its weight in her hand. Not the best stake, but it would do. Hopefully.

Normally in a situation like this, Harper would let Romeo go after the vamp first, then help him if necessary. After all, slayers, even crappy ones like Romeo, were ten times stronger than the average human, and unfortunately, being a seer didn't afford her any supernatural strength.

But Romeo—the rat bastard—was probably at the Bellagio, hip-deep in hookers and craps winnings at the moment.

Harper heard the woman scream as she kicked the back door open and stumbled into the alley.

Just like in her premonition, a biker-clad vampire had the small woman pinned up against the dumpster with the weight of his body, one beefy arm across her shoulders, his other hand clutching her jaw so that he had a clear shot at her jugular.

Harper's heart clawed its way up to her throat as she met the woman's horror-filled gaze. She could practically taste the woman's fear.

She swallowed hard and forced herself to break eye contact, taking stock of the situation. Her gaze flicked over the vampire.

The vamp had at least eight inches and a hundred pounds on her. This could be a problem, common sense told her.

But as usual, her mouth didn't listen to common sense. "Hey, asshole."

The vampire raised his head from the woman's throat, a crimson ribbon of blood dribbling down his chin. Cute.

"Why don't you pick on someone more my size."

Okay, so it was a line she'd picked up from watching Buffy the Vampire Slayer reruns. Witty repartee should never be wasted, even if it wasn't original.

He laughed, a hollow, cold sound that slithered up and down her spine, leaving goose bumps in its wake. "Run while you still can, little girl."

She shook her head and clucked her tongue. "I don't think so, Vlad. Running? Not so much a good idea in these shoes."

His fangs slowly retracted like a cat's claws, making him look almost human. Almost.

"I like a girl with spirit," he said. "Enhances her flavor."

"Wow, that was almost clever. I'm shocked. I had you pegged as stupid and ugly. Maybe I can upgrade you to just ugly."

Harper had forgotten how fast a motivated vampire could move. One second he was ten feet away, and half a heartbeat later, he stood close enough to backhand her.

And backhand her he did. For him it was careless, effortless. Like swatting a fly. It was still enough to fill her mouth with blood and knock her on her ass.

From her position on the ground, she noticed the blond still frozen in place against the dumpster. "Run," she mouthed.

Obviously in shock, the blond stared at her as if she hadn't noticed, and this time Harper shouted, "Run!"

The girl finally seemed to snap out of her stupor. She spun on her heel and fled down the alley.

Harper breathed a sigh of relief as she shakily climbed to her feet and faced a very large, very angry vampire.

Yipes.

"Bitch," he said through clenched teeth, "I'm gonna take you apart piece by piece."

Again, common sense wasn't Harper's co-pilot as she spat back, "Gee, that might be scary if I didn't already know you hit like a girl."

This time when he swung at her, she was ready for him. Harper kicked out as he lunged for her, catching him in the knee with her gold platforms.

He went down with a yelp. "You bitch!"

"Now, I'm getting real sick of you calling me that."

Harper tried to kick him in the face, but he was too fast for her. He grabbed her ankle and yanked it out from under her. She landed on her butt with an unladylike grunt.

God, where was a good crossbow when she really needed one?

He was on her before she could scramble to her feet, pinning her to the ground with his weight. She managed to free one of her hands and gouged his eye, gagging a little as her thumb sunk in up to the knuckle.

The vampire screeched and leapt off her, one hand pressed to what was left of his eye.

Harper stood up and raised the stake. "Now, I don't want to kill you, but I will if I have to. If you run away now, we can forget this whole thing ever happened."

He whipped a wicked-looking hunting knife out of his jacket pocket. "You're gonna die slow."

Harper took a big step back. So much for diplomacy.

But before she could come up with any other bright ideas, someone moved up fast behind her and shoved her out of the way. She hit the ground again.

Being a hero certainly wasn't all it was cracked up to be. Very hard on the tush.

"Who the fuck are you?" the vamp yelled, clutching the knife in one hand and his eye with the other.

"Death," the newcomer answered dryly.

Harper's head shot up. She'd know that voice anywhere.

Standing a few feet away from her, presenting her with his impressive profile, was Mr. Congeniality himself: the gorgeous, potential serial-killer from table five.

On a happier note, Harper realized that Mr. Personality was at least a head taller than the vamp and seemed to have more muscle weight. That might even the odds a little for the home team, she decided.

The vamp took a step back and raised his hands, suddenly all friendly and peace-loving. "Look, man, I got no problem with you."

Harper snorted. "Who's the bitch now, you big pussy?"

She slapped a hand over her mouth. Damn it, she hadn't meant to say that out loud.

Her savior glanced over at her and that was all the time the vamp needed. He swung out wildly, slicing neatly into Table Five's stomach. Harper gasped as blood quickly dampened the fabric of his T-shirt.

But the wound didn't even seem to faze Table Five. He caught the vamp's fist when he took his next shot and used his momentum to pull him closer, then drove his knee into the vampire's stomach. The vampire dropped to his knees, arms wrapped around his middle as he coughed and gagged. Table Five kicked out without hesitation, catching the vamp in the chin, knocking him flat on his back.

Table Five yanked him up by the hair and twisted his arm behind his back. A sound akin to a dry twig snapping was closely followed by another pained groan from the vampire.

Harper blinked. It took a hell of a lot of strength to break a vampire's bones. An unnatural amount of strength. This guy did it without even trying. Who the hell was he?

"Quit whining," Table Five growled at the now blubbering vampire, then gave him a good swift kick in the ass. "And get the hell out of here while I'm still in a good mood."

Harper kept her eyes on the vamp until he'd stumbled out of view, then turned her attention to the man who'd saved her life. The man who'd just reduced a violent vampire to tears.

"Who are you?" she asked suspiciously. "And don't say Death."

He glanced at her and the street light allowed her to see his eyes were blue. Deep, deep blue. Gorgeous, she thought, then mentally slapped herself for noticing something so trivial after what had just happened.

He paused as if contemplating not telling her his name, but eventually said, "Call me Riddick."

Harper realized she was still on the ground and slowly climbed to her feet. All her parts seemed to be in working order, and she hadn't peed herself. She supposed she couldn't really ask for more than that, given the circumstances.

"Riddick?" she repeated. "Like the Vin Diesel movies?"

He stared at her like she was deranged. Must not be a Vin Diesel fan.

Then it occurred to her where she'd heard the name before, and Vin Diesel had nothing to do with it. "Are you Noah Riddick? The slayer?"

He wadded up the fabric at the hem of his T-shirt and pressed it to his wound. "There aren't any more slayers."

She rolled her eyes. Slayers and seers hadn't fallen off the face of the earth when Sentry disbanded and vamps earned human rights. They might be jobless, but they still existed. "I'm thinking the vamp with the broken arm still believes in slayers."

Noah Riddick in Whispering Hope, Harper thought when he didn't respond. What were the odds?

Whispering Hope had been settled largely by Italian, Polish and Irish immigrants who hadn't enjoyed big city life, which accounted for the fact that there were a ton of great restaurants in her beloved town, but no industry to speak of. And it was too far away from the real city for convenience, so truly, the only reason Harper could think of for anyone who wasn't born in Whispering Hope to settle here was the food.

But she'd just bet that Noah Riddick wasn't in town for a kolache from Majesky's on High Street.

Riddick adjusted his makeshift compress and she stared at his bare stomach, not sure if she was more fascinated by the wound—which was pumping out a surprising amount of blood—or by his perfect abs.

She cleared her throat. "We should probably get you to a hospital. That stomach looks hot…er, I mean it looks like it hurts."

Sweet Christ, could she humiliate herself in front of this guy a few more times?

"I don't do hospitals," he said.

Great. A macho man. Just what she needed more of in her life. "Okay, so, if you don't do hospitals, do you bleed to death in alleys? 'Cause if that's what you're going for, you're well on your way, dude." She gave him a thumbs-up. "Way to go."

His gaze moved over her and he shook his head. He shrugged out of his coat and tossed it to her, grimacing.

"Put it on," he said. "I can't even hear myself think over the sound of your teeth chattering."

"Gee, and they say chivalry is dead," she intoned dryly, shoving her arms into the sleeves of the black trench.

The coat was too long by nearly a foot, and the sleeves hung down well below her hands, but the fabric still held the warmth of his skin, and she was far too cold to be concerned with fit or fashion. The What Not to Wear folks could just kiss her warm, toasty ass.

He watched her fidget for a while before asking, "Who are you?"

"I'm Harper." She shook the sleeves of the coat back, finally finding her hand and extending it to him. "Harper Hall."

He stared at her hand, then raised his gaze to hers. "That

explains a lot."

Harper let her hand sink back into the coat's depths and narrowed her eyes on him. "What's that supposed to mean?"

"You were Romeo Jones' seer. That explains why you were willing to take off, alone, after a vamp three-times your size with a chair leg." His gaze moved over her again, slowly. "In your underwear."

She put her hand on her hip and cocked her head to one side. "Are you insulting me, or are you insulting Romeo? Because if you're insulting me, you and I need to have a serious come-to-Jesus meeting."

For a split second, he looked like he might smile, but just when she was deciding whether to go after him with her make-shift stake or chick-fight him with her fingernails, the smile died and pain flashed through his eyes.

"Let's just say your reputation precedes you," he said, hunching over almost imperceptibly.

Hmmpphh. Noah Riddick talking trash about her reputation. Wasn't that just rich beyond belief?

"Well, hello there, Pot, they call me Kettle," she said dryly. "I hear you're black."

He raised one eyebrow and took a step toward her, only to

sway drunkenly before falling to his knees. "Fuck," he muttered, one hand on the ground, one hand on his stomach.

Harper rushed to his side, but he stopped her with a fierce scowl. "I'm not Romeo," he hissed. "I don't need your help."

She straightened and planted her hands on her hips again. "Look, I've taken about all the shit I intend to from you. So, as I see it, you've got two choices: you can lay there and bleed to death, or you can suck up your stupid male pride and let me help you."

He looked at her like he'd rather rip his heart out with his bare hands than accept her help, but after what must have been an exhausting battle of pride and necessity, he allowed her to ease her shoulder under his arm and help him stand.

Leaning heavily on her, he whispered, "No hospitals," right before he passed out.

Harper staggered under his weight, but somehow managed to keep them both vertical. After a moment of struggling and cussing, she was able to lean him against the dumpster and hold him upright with her bodyweight while she mulled her options.

He didn't want to go to the hospital, and probably rightfully so.

If there were any pro-vamp zealots out there looking for a little slayer-bashing action, he'd be a sitting duck in the hospital.

She couldn't take him back into the Kitty Kat Palace. Bleeding men tended to draw attention there as well.

That really only left one viable option.

Boy, if Riddick thought she was reckless now, wait until he woke up in her bed.

Like it so far? The entire Harper Hall Investigations series is now available just about everywhere books are sold! Here's the reading order:

Semi-Charmed

Semi-Human

Semi-Twisted

Semi-Broken

Semi-Sane

The Harper Hall Investigations complete series boxset

Made in the USA
Coppell, TX
29 July 2020

32038603R00175